Cleo's Oak

A NOVEL BY

Pearle Munn Bishop

Willow's Page

❧⚜

I hate it, I hate it, I hate it. I could write I hate it five hundred times and I would still hate it.

Cleo has forced me to spend my whole sixteenth summer telling her story. If I had wanted to tell a story it would be about myself. I am, first of all, beautiful. Everyone says so and I know it is true. I look like a young edition of the models you see on television and in magazines. I am five feet ten inches tall, weigh one hundred and twenty pounds. I have thick hair and long legs.

My background is German-Lutheran, but my family on my mother's side has been American for at least six generations. I have had everything money and prestige can give a girl in sixteen years—private schools, tutors, dance, music, tennis, golf, and skiing. Maybe I am vain but I have lots of friends and I was happy until one day everything changed.

While playing Frisbee with my younger brother, I fell and hit the back of my head on a rock. The blow knocked me unconscious for less than a minute. My mother was frantic. Doctor Johnson told her I seemed to just have a lump on the back of my head, for her to watch me for nausea, slurred speech, unresponsiveness, and for me to get some rest.

Sleep came easy. My dreams were about people, mostly

women in old-fashioned clothes. My mother must have called everyone she knew. Although I was at home, I received flowers from ten people and cards and email from people I hardly knew.

One thing I have always done is to write thank you notes as quickly as possible. When I started to write my first note, the words were not mine. They were about canning peaches, back porches, cows, pigs, then something about playing baseball. This was the beginning of the story you are reading. I had become a channeler for Cleo.

My sixteenth summer was spent at my computer. I pray that Cleo is the only spirit that will use me to tell her story. I am not a part of her story—or perhaps I am.

Willow

❧❦

Cleo's Oak

Chapter 1: To Willow

Willow, I am Cleo. I want you to write my story.

My father Alexander Lamb came to America in the year 1844 at age sixteen working his way across the Atlantic on a sailing ship. His Scottish family was large and poor. His mother had second sight and predicted great things for the new country, America, although she never told Alexander if his future was revealed to her.

In New York, Alexander found other people from the Isle of Bute and got a job with the city, building roads. He was restless. For a while he helped build sailing ships, then went to work in stables caring for horses.

A local policeman's daughter, Rosa MacRay, kept her horse in this stable. My mother's father was a hard-boiled, ambitious, angry Irishman that did not want his only daughter to become involved with a ne'er-do-well Scot who couldn't hold a job and worked at a horse stable. Somehow, the young lovers found a way to be together. Sometimes they met on a rooftop, and as my father told me later, "they were married in the sight of God," on a rooftop.

My mother convinced friends to help them elope, and he married Rosa MacRay, the policeman's daughter. I was born seven and a half months after the marriage. My mother must have been a romantic to name me Cleopatra. I have no memory of that period, of course, only what my father told me later. When I was about two years old, my mother died in childbirth. The stillborn baby boy was buried with her. After my mother's death, my grandparents wanted to take me to raise. My father was afraid if he refused, he would wind up dead. Since my grandfather was a New York policeman, my father was sure he could find a way to kill him and suffer no repercussions.

Then started our period of wandering. My father's feet were made for leaving, but he never left me but once. I was always a big, big part of who he was. He was a large, quiet, handsome man, a nice shy smile and he was always loving and protecting me. He was a listener—spoke only when he had something important to say. He read stories to me until I learned to read. Then I read to him. We sat for hours. I would sit on his lap or at his feet, wherever the light was better. He would hug me, touch my face or arms, and play with my hair.

His jobs were varied. Sometimes we would live in town, sometimes in the country, nice houses or shacks. Early during the time my father was working, I would stay with different families. When he was off work, we were together. I went to so many different schools I lost count.

At my first school on the first school day I talked a lot. No one, not even father, had ever told me to shut up. Other children were talking as much as I. We got through one day, then the teacher took charge. Rule one, stay in your seat. Rule two, talk only when asked to by the teacher. Rule three, if you must speak, hold up your right hand. She had to teach most of us which was our right hand and what the other one was called.

On the playground at recess, the teacher came over to the swing I was using, caught the rope, took hold of my shoulders with both hands, looked me straight in the eyes and said, "You are a challenge."

Challenge was a new word for me. I quit talking for the rest of the day. Later, Father listened to my stories of the day, smiled and said very little until I got to the word, "challenge."

Then he told me about his childhood. He had been sent to a Catholic boarding school before he was two, had become a ward of the Church and cared for in a group of other children by two Greek nuns. His mother requested he be given lessons in swimming. If she gave the Priest a reason, my father was never told. He wondered if she had known he would cross the Atlantic as a sailor. He became a strong swimmer and loved the water.

The Priest taught him English and Latin. The Sisters taught him Greek. He also took classes in Hebrew, theology, rhetoric, composition, mathematics, public speaking, chemistry, astronomy, philosophy, history and law. He retained most everything he was taught. The whole school considered him a "challenge," he was such a good student.

When father was sixteen, the nuns went back to Greece and he knew he did not want to become a priest. The Priest gave him new clothes and a small amount of money. His mother gave him a scarf she had woven from wool she had gathered on the farm where they lived. She also gave him a small green stone. He visited his family, said good-bye and went to sea. Until then, I had not realized the medical books I was taught to read were Latin and the beautiful book about the Greek Gods was Greek. The Bible was English. I made up my mind to always be a "challenge."

Father and I fished, swam and rode horses together. We ran instead of walked. We had runs down miles and miles of country roads.

He loved me; I could not wait to spend time with him. As I became older I hung around his place of work. I rode horses, learned to care for them, drove the buggies, whatever I could do to be close to him. We always had a good horse and wagon.

Talk—my mouth ran all my waking hours. If no one was around, I talked to the trees. "The moss on your north side is really thick this year. Does that mean a cold winter is coming?"

The beauty of talking to the trees is they talk back. This I would do with rocks, chicks, people, dolls—whatever or whoever was around. Not only would I talk, I would listen. I knew secrets, some I was told, some I just knew. Sometimes knowing made me happy. Other times I would rather not know.

When I was about six, I told a woman I hardly knew that her three-year-old son would be washed away in the river and when his body was found, it would be eaten away by fish and turtles. This I had seen in a vision. I had not only seen it, I heard it, I smelled it—the water in the river was cold. What an uproar that caused. When three weeks later what I had told the mother came true, even I was frightened.

How did I know this? Were all the things that filtered through my brain true? That shipwreck I "saw," did it really happen? I knew that old lady Pridgen was going to die on Sunday, but most anyone else could figure that out. Maybe not see her as I did in her death bed and hear her last gasp of air, but surely everybody knew her time was near.

After the death of the three-year-old boy, some people wanted me to tell them "things." Other people would cross the road and hide when I was near. No one would look me in the eye.

Soon after that, one Friday, Father said it was time to move on. We packed our covered wagon with food, clothes, pots, pans, books, saddles and hay. Sometimes when we moved the people would give us a party. Not this time. The only gift I received was an all-black, five-week-old kitten. The five-year-old brother of the boy that drowned met our wagon about two miles down the road. Without a word, he handed her to me. I took her. No one spoke. I did not learn if she was a gift from the mother or the boy.

I named her Friday. From then on, Friday and I seemed attached to each other. I had heard tales of witches and black cats but I knew I was not a witch. Witches were old crones with big noses, warts and hunched backs. They boiled things in pots. The things I boiled in pots were good to eat or maybe the kettle would hold our clothes boiled to get clean.

Chapter 2

*D*id I tell you about my father's love of animals and plants? Our food always tasted good because we gathered herbs, berries, sweet smelling twigs, and fungi to add to the pot of meat my father or I trapped. We ate rabbit, squirrel, deer, wild pig or things father brought home from his job. Some summers we planted a garden and preserved what we did not use.

My brain was pretty quick—if I heard it once, it stayed with me. The value of herbs in cooking led to the value of herbs in healing. In time people seemed to treat me as a shadow of my father and forget I was there. Mostly girls were not allowed around the barn during the conception and birth of animals and during the veterinarian's treatments of sick animals. I was not only there, my hands helped catch the newborn. My hands guided their mouths to their first taste of sweet milk. In all of this, the love my father and I had for each other was a constant.

Father was a good hired hand. He was never fired. We just moved on—sometimes at the end of a season, sometimes after a year, sometimes with another job waiting, sometimes, I suspect, because he thought agents of my grandfather might be closing in. One winter we spent in a cave in the woods. That was so good. We were warm and dry—did lots of fishing, trapping and reading. Always our supply of books went with us. The Bible, Shakespeare, our medical books, books about the Greek Gods, a Latin dictionary and many more. Our horse must have hated the load he had to pull in that heavy wagon.

Friday went with us everywhere. I carried her, sometimes on my back, sometimes on my stomach. I said she was "riding on my heart" when she was on my stomach.

The cave was much deeper than we were able to explore. We tied vines together to make a long rope, then explored in the dark until we ran out of the rope. Lighting our torches, we went to the end of the new rope we had attached, put out our torches and, using the rope as a guide, returned to our camp in the entrance of the cave. We found remains of old campfires deep in the cave.

Once we saw the skeletons of two bodies high on a ledge. Why they went so high up in the ceiling of that cave to die we did not know. We could tell they were Indian by the bits of leather clothing we found. I picked up a small piece of the leather and tucked it into the pouch on my stomach with Friday.

That night, cuddled up in a blanket with Father and Friday, I took the piece of leather in my hands and started talking. Where those words came from I do not know but I am sure they were the truth. About the bodies on the ledge, I spoke of an old, old Indian man and his old, old wife. Knowing their time on earth was ending, they went alone together to a ledge in the cave they had selected many years before. They lay down together and began their death chant. Their passing was peaceful. He went first. She watched his spirit rise and float over her. She knew he was waiting for her. She sang the death chant five more times and her spirit joined his. It was a joyful reunion.

The next day we took the small piece of leather back to the ledge.

We were not completely isolated in our cave. There was a small town about an hour's ride away. That's where we sold the game we killed and the hides we dressed. Father and I rode double with me in front. The horse seemed to enjoy the trips to town as much as we did. We bought only what we really needed and told no one where we were living. Father was the best teacher I could have had. School was wherever we were, in the cave, the woods or riding our horse.

Spirituality, not religion was what grounded my father. He believed in God, Jesus, the Greek Gods, the Roman Gods, the God in the oak trees, Mother Nature, Mother Earth, Buddha and others. He thought we inherited our religion as we inherited our blue eyes. To him our spirit was ours alone. Sundays were holy days. If there was a church nearby, we attended it. At some churches, men sat on the right hand side and women and children on the left. Father and I always sat together, holding hands most of the time. We both sang with spirit and good voice.

If there was no church and we were alone on Sunday, we would go to our oak tree and have our private service. Our oak tree stood out from the other trees in the forest. It was the largest and the most perfect tree we could find near our cave. A short distance away from this great oak we put a circle of stones. Each of the thirteen stones had a base of about thirteen inches long. These stones were placed three inches apart. The theory was if we sat within this circle and asked the God of the Oak to help us find direction for our lives, we would be advised what to do.

We never stepped into the "magic" circle. I trusted Father to guide us in the direction we should go. I led the service and sometimes I made it very long, with many songs or reciting long poems in any of the three languages I knew, English, Greek or Latin. Other times our service would be short. Once I repeated the prayer an old man had used three months before in a church we had visited. This prayer was about half an hour long. The old man was really shaking when he finally finished. Father was quiet, his prayers unspoken.

I could have been happy in that cave forever but spring came and we moved on. I wanted to take our circle of stones with us but Father said, "We will build another. This magic circle may help someone who needs it more than we do."

I hope our circle works magic for someone looking for direction for their life. Maybe they will find our cave. We left pots, pans and dishes. The pots were sooted from the outside fire and the dishes mismatched. We knew we would not need them. Our new place would have all the kitchen things we needed. I even left the doll a shopkeeper's daughter had given me.

We were in town one day when the man who bought our produce said there was a man staying at the hotel that was looking for a farm hand. We went to see him. Father told him we would need a house; that he couldn't just live in a bunk house with a child. That is when we met Mr. Stuart and made the move to Arcidia, Indiana. This was just before my tenth birthday.

The Stuart family was expecting us when we arrived on a Friday afternoon. The sun was shining and my smile was bright, my dress clean, my hair brushed. Honestly, I did not know how to brush my hair; Father did that many times a day. At night he would brush it and plait it, "so the witches would not play with it," he said.

The Stuart clan was busy with whatever cow people do in the afternoon on a farm. Missus Stuart and the housekeeper, Missus Bell, came to our wagon and invited us in for tea. Tea consisted of the best apple strudel I had ever tasted plus some kind of tea that was black and did not smell nearly as good as the tea Father and I made from the twigs and barks we found in the woods. Father drank it anyway. I had milk. I was rather starved for milk. We had taken a milk goat to our cave and still had her in our wagon but she had quit producing milk in mid-winter and was ready for breeding. I missed having her milk. I had two and one half glasses of thick rich cow's milk each day the rest of my life.

Over on a small hill not too far from the Stuart home was a small, unpainted house. After about an hour for tea, Missus Stuart directed us toward this house and said, "Welcome home. I hope you will be happy here for many years."

Never will I forget the welcome this house gave me. Getting out of the wagon, I turned around. The building seemed to have arms that reached out and embraced me. Father was still working with the reins of the horse and did not seem to experience this embrace. There was even a small barn and garden space as part of the house plot.

I ran with joy to the steps, on to the porch, opened the screen door, and stepped inside. Happiness overwhelmed me. I spun round and around till I was dizzy. I would have kept spinning except Father caught me in the middle of a spin and hugged me. The smile on his face was no longer shy. To see me so happy, his smile went from ear to ear.

I had loved my winter in the cave. There, I had felt safe, secure, spiritual, treasured. Always treasured, never did I doubt my worth. I knew I was God's child or maybe I belonged to the spirit of the oak tree.

Here in this small house in the open meadow there was joy, freedom. The whole world was just outside the door. Inside that door was "home."

It was not so grand as the Stuart house, which was not really grand, just a rambling farm house built on and up for three generations. It now housed the man, his wife, three girls with brown eyes, three boys with blue eyes, Missus Bell and her fourteen-year-old grandson.

Our house was different. There were five steps leading to a porch that went all the way round the house. I mean you could start running round and round and never stop. It had three outside doors—one in the front, one facing the garden area and one in the back facing the barn.

The windows were small, eight of them, nine if you counted the weird glass space in the attic that would not open. That attic got hot enough to fry an egg in the summer. Oh, well, it was still spring and I had a real stove to fry my eggs. For the last six months, our eggs had been fried, boiled, or scrambled over a fire we built either inside the mouth of our cave, if it was raining or snowing, or outside in the open. We had taken five hens with us when we moved into the cave. No roosters. We knew we would be cooking those hens before we moved on. There was no need for fertile eggs. At night we took those hens into the cave with us. We planned to eat them, not let some of those wild creatures get what we had fed and protected.

The great room in our new home had a big fireplace with an oven built into the wall. The fireplace had four hooks for hanging pots and pots a-plenty were on the hearth. To the left of the fireplace was this beautiful iron stove. It was a little rusty. In fact the whole house needed a little cleaning.

I looked forward to making that place mine. I figured in two days it would look like a different place. An old brick and a little effort would make that stove shine and that wood floor smooth. There was a small table with a flour bin at the end. An open shelf on the wall held two rolling pins, iron fry pans, white ironstone dishes—more dishes than two people would ever use. The last hired hand must have had a passel of children.

Built into the wall of the great room were two bunk beds. The curtains that covered them were not too clean but were made of good homespun. I knew a good wash was all they needed.

The big table could hold twelve people easily. I would be using my brick on that table top also, maybe even on the legs. Pushed under that table were two benches that would hold six people each. Also in the room were two wing chairs, looking really ratty. How I was going to improve those I did not know. Hanging about halfway up the wall were five straight chairs. All of this furniture had a homemade look, even the stuffed chairs. Everything we needed seemed to be there.

Father and I moved the things from the wagon that went into the house. The goat and two hens went into the barn and chicken yard. Oh, you thought we had eaten all those hens. Those two never did get eaten. They died of old age. Did you know that old chicken hens look like old chicken hens. They lose some of their feathers and limp around dragging their wings. They really become tough old birds.

There were three doors in the wall behind the fireplace. We knew they must lead into small bedrooms. The doors were all closed.

Father said, "You open one and I will open the other. If there are any ghosts sleeping, we will surprise them."

On the count of three we opened the two doors furthest away

from the chimney. No ghosts. Mine had two single beds, a chest, and a long board nailed to the wall with six iron hooks attached. An old red jacket hung on one of the hooks. A badly damaged book lay on the small square table between the beds. Someone had placed a beautifully designed bird's nest on the shelf.

I ran over to see what Father had found. His room had a double bed, a dresser with a mirror, a wash stand with bowl and pitcher. There was still some water in the pitcher. Plus a shelf and a board with hooks like in the room I had explored.

The room behind the fireplace had yet to be revealed. I opened the door and went in. Father followed. This was the best bedroom. It had a small fireplace, a three-quarter bed with the ropes real tight. The bed was made up with two quilts plus a hand-woven, blue and white wool cover. The chest at the end of the bed was oak, made with loving hands. A dresser held a lamp, hand mirror, and three small hand-carved boxes. The painting on the wall was of a small, slightly hunchback woman smiling. There was not a trace of lint or dust anywhere. No ashes in the fireplace. Beautifully cut small logs lay there with precise layered kindling.

This was a shrine. I was not ready to find out to whom. Someday I thought I might return and open the oak chest. We backed out of the room, closed the door and did not speak of what we had seen until winter started again.

Willow, I want to address you directly. Have you gotten all of this down? Do not leave out anything. Each person, each place, each event is important. This is my story. The people you will meet will only be the ones important to my story. I want certain rules followed. Do not use numbers for letters, if I say three, write three. Do not use contractions. Your spelling should always be correct. I will forgive phrases of yours that will better convey my story, but learn how to use correct punctuation so readers will understand.

Back to my story.

Chapter 3

*M*issus Bell had given us a basket of food. Tea with Missus Stuart and her had been satisfying, so we decided to wait until evening to eat again. I could not wait to build a fire in that iron stove. So I did. I put water in a pot to heat with the idea of cleaning something.

Father went out toward the barn to look for Mister Stuart. Watching him walk toward the barn I realized it had been hours since I answered a call of nature. You would say "went to the bathroom." There was never a place to take a bath in the little houses "out back," just one or two holes to relieve oneself. As I watched Father walk toward the barn, I located our outhouse. Someone had planted shrubs that were blooming with yellow blossoms. I had never seen a prettier outhouse although I could just see part of the top because of the blossoms. My plan was to ask what was the name of the plant.

When I returned to the house, the water was hot on the stove. I was really glad Father had gotten me three buckets of water from the spring on the far end of the garden before he went to the barn. There was in the kitchen area a metal sink, one and one half feet by three feet, plus a pitcher pump for water, but the pump had to be primed and I didn't want to wait for that to be done. Six cakes of yellow soap wrapped in oiled paper sat high on a shelf in the kitchen. I had to take down one of the straight chairs from the wall to stand on to get the soap.

I scrubbed the small kitchen table and the big table. The iron kettle, Dutch oven and fry pans I cleaned with scouring brush and sand. Four lamps were lined up on a shelf in the kitchen, two full of coal oil, two about half full so I knew when it got full dark we would have plenty of light for our reading.

Father wanted me to have the bedroom with the full size bed, but I pointed out to him how big he was and how small I was. Sometimes I think he forgets I am nine years old going on ten. So we decided I would have the bedroom with the two single beds.

Cleaning and making his bed was easy. Together we had washed our sheets, blankets, towels and clothes before we had left our cave. I mostly just fixed his bed, then went into my room and made up one of the single beds. I put our best blanket over the other bed just to make the room look nice.

It was about dark when Father came back. He was pleased with all the cleaning I had done. He said he met Mister Stuart and two of his hired hands. I found out later there were four hired hands who lived in the bunk house.

We opened up the supper basket Missus Bell had packed for us, found a baked hen, a quart jar of butterbeans, a quart of canned tomatoes, a loaf of bread, a pound of butter and a small jar of blackberry preserves.

I sprinkled the top of the bread with water, popped it into the oven for a few minutes, warmed the vegetables on the stove, then we started eating. The bread smelled so good we could not wait to butter it and eat. Now, the chicken and butterbeans were not as good as they could have been. Had I been cooking the hen, I would have used more pepper, more sage or rosemary. Maybe Missus Bell would teach me to make bread and I would teach her to use herbs.

After dinner Father and I were both tired and skipped our usual reading. When I went to bed, I took Friday with me. She had been asleep most of the day on top of one of the stuffed chairs. We decided to leave the two straight chairs off their hooks. They looked nice just where we used them at supper.

After I had been in bed about an hour without sleeping, I re-

21

membered the bunk beds in the great room. Picking up Friday, my pillow and blanket, I crept out of my room to the lower bunk and in a few minute, I was asleep. That bunk became my bed. I felt I was in the embrace of my new home.

The next morning Father and I went out to find a replacement for our oak tree we had left near the cave. There were many trees. We picked the most perfect oak tree in the woods. It was in deep woods but no other trees had crowded this one. We did not find all thirteen stones to make our circle that day.

Father let me pick out the stones and I was very particular. I said, "Each stone has to tell me it is a magic stone and that it belongs in our circle."

It took us about three weeks before we were satisfied we had created a truly magic circle. We did not step into it. We just wanted it in reserve waiting for us if we ever felt we needed direction for our lives.

Maybe I should tell you more about the Stuarts as they became a large part of my story. Mister Stuart's grandfather came to America sometime in the late seventeen hundreds and started the farm. He had one son, Daniel. Daniel married Ruth Franklin. Ruth's family owned much land with mineral rights in Virginia's coal country. From that marriage on, money was never a problem for the Stuarts. Ruth and Daniel had one son that they named Daniel the sixth, as there had been other Daniel Stuarts in Scotland. Daniel the sixth was our Mister Stuart. Mister Stuart married Grace Grayson, also from Virginia, a daughter of one of his Virginia family friends—our Missus Stuart.

Together they had six children, three girls and three boys. The girls had brown eyes like their mother, the boys blue eyes like their father. First in eighteen hundred and forty came Lily Lea. Lily Lea was seventeen when my father and I moved to the Stuart farm and she was a student at Missus Howard's finishing school. We saw her only for two weeks in July of the year eighteen hundred and fifty-eight. Daniel Samuel was born four years after Lily. He was a tall, very serious, caring boy. Daniel spent most of his spare time sketching, painting, or wood carving. He and Ole Joe —one of the farm hands—would sit and whittle for hours. Ole Joe liked to carve cows. Daniel mostly carved horses.

Two years later came my favorite, Rosa Ellen, who had beautiful dark brown hair and a bouncy outlook on life. A year older than me, she was looking for a "best friend." The first words I said to her were, "My mother's name was Rosa." That sealed our friendship for both of us.

James Powell was born in eighteen-forty-nine. He just butted into everything Rosa and I wanted to do. He was a nuisance. The two younger children, Annie Margaret, four, and David Thomas, three, played together most of the time. Annie seemed to think D.T., as he was called, was her baby.

The rest of the household consisted of Missus Bell and her grandson, Jed. Missus Bell had been the Stuarts' housekeeper before the present Stuarts were married and had cared for her grandson, Jed, since his mother died at his birth. Jed was fourteen when we moved to the farm. When he was not Mister Stuarts' "right hand man," he was doing something Missus Bell wanted him to do. He grew up on the farm, slept in the house, ate with the family, went with them to the same church on Sunday. He did most of the things the rest of the family did. But his heart was on the farm. Someday he wanted to own his own farm and have more beef cattle than Mister Stuart.

At times when guests were expected at roundup or harvest time, other women would come in to help Missus Bell. The family members did their part also. Each person made their own bed and straightened up their bedroom before they left it for breakfast. While at our house after my father and I had breakfast, I would straighten up our house before going over to do whatever Missus Bell or Missus Stuart would ask me to do. Rosa and I made short work of that house cleaning. If we were told to go outside and pick beans, cucumbers or whatever, we did it as fast as we could. I talked; Rosa giggled; we danced. It was a fun, fun summer.

That summer passed quickly. Only two outstanding things happened, well, three if you count my birthday. Oh yes, let us count my birthday. I was ten years old July second. First let me tell you about Father teaching all the Stuart clan to swim really well. Actually he taught most all the neighborhood —except Missus Bell. She said, "I have been cold and wet and do not want that to happen again."

The swimming hole had been used since the area was settled by the pioneers. Men and boys from miles around came after work, or maybe snuck off even before their chores were finished, to swim.

The first day of May my father and I started to the swimming hole. The word got out that a "girl" was coming to this all male place. We could hear the complaints before we even got near the river. When we arrived there were only three males in the water and they were wearing long johns, a winter type of underwear, which is what my father wore to swim. The others were hiding in the woods getting dressed. I had made a swimming costume like one I had seen in a magazine.

The water was cold. We entered the water slowly as we did not know the depth. There was a shelf on the bottom of the river for about thirty feet, then it dropped off fast. If you went beyond that thirty feet, you better know how to swim. Father and I had been swimming together since I could remember, so the depth did not matter. But if we did not want to be swept downstream, we had to stay out of the swift current.

I think both my father and I started showing off a little. I was so proud of our ability to swim better than the others there. It was really cold so none of us stayed in the water long.

Missus Stuart, among others, heard about our swimming ability and asked my father if he would teach her family to swim. It was decided to make Wednesday afternoons "Ladies Day." Most all the females and small children except Missus Bell met at the swimming hole just after twelve on Wednesdays. Father was the teacher, and I helped with the young ones. Before the summer was over, we had some really great swimmers in that group. Missus Stuart could swim a little before this. She had been taught at Missus Howard's finishing school. That summer she learned to swim really well.

The males got their swimming hole back on the other days. I did not go with my father swimming again when just males were present. He also taught the males to swim and they taught others. I bet people in that part of Indiana are good swimmers today because father started that class.

The fair came to Arcidia July first and stayed five days. One thing that had always made me feel special was that America seemed to be ready to party the week of my birthday, July second. This year was my tenth birthday and the whole town seemed to be celebrating.

Father and I had been to fairs before and looked at cows, horses, chickens, plows and other farm type things. We walked the Midway, ate different types of foods. But this year was different. I was given money and told to go and have a good time with my friends. Having close girl friends was new to me. My four "best friends"—Rosa was the very best— and I went straight to the Midway.

There were three tents with weird people in them. There was a family of tiny people; the man and woman were not as tall as my waist. The two children were smaller yet. We found out later they were not really a "family." The man was from somewhere in Europe. The woman was married to the man that took tickets at the front gate. He was as tall as most men. The children had been given to the owner of the fair by their parents.

We saw a calf with two heads that was dead and had been stuffed with straw. That was really no big deal. On the farm where my father worked when I was seven and a half, a colt had been delivered with two heads.

Later we went to see the judging of the baked goods, the quilts, canned stuff, flowers and so forth. Most everybody from the Stuart farm had entered something. Mine was a pie. Missus Bell was the only one to win a blue ribbon and she won four, two for her breads, one for her pie, and one for a walnut cake.

Then we went to watch the games. In horseback riding we thought our farm hands looked the best, but they were beaten by the boys from the Stonewall farm. Our boys won in pitching horseshoes and harness pull. Lily looked so beautiful and proud as she showed her horse. She won in her class. She should have, most everyone on the farm for the last month had groomed that horse. Lily's riding outfit had been made special for her in New York City.

One thing we did not watch was the raw egg eating contest. There were only two farm hands entered and the betting was heavy. The winner ate four dozen and two raw eggs in ten minutes. The other cowboy ate four dozen. Missus Stuart would not allow any of our farm eggs to be sold for two weeks before the fair. She wanted to have no part of that contest. Before the last egg was eaten, the loser was behind the tent, vomiting. The winner was close behind him. The cheers from the men that bet on the winner were loud and the event was talked about in the bunk houses until the next fair when two other farm hands tried to beat the record.

The Fourth of July gala had been in the planning stage for over a year. Mister Muller, the owner of the largest store in Arcidia and Missus Stuart planned the gala. Two musician friends of Mister Muller came for a two month visit the last of May. Mister Muller's original home had been Wurzburg, Germany, the heart of the wine country. His friends brought the wine, Hochheimer, Steinwein, and a sweet Beerenauslesen for the gala.

During the month of June, they practiced with the local band the sophisticated music for the dances. Missus Stuart and the Mullers had been teaching the local people these dances for a year. It turned out to be a grand affair. Missus Bell remodeled an emerald green and white ball gown of Lily's for me. It was my first dress-up dress. Missus Stuart's dressmaker made a lovely yellow gown for Rosa. Rosa had dress-up clothes since she was born. Missus Stuart wore the gown she had used at her graduation from Missus Howard's Finishing School many years before. Using a little powder and staining her cheeks and lips with crushed rose petals, she looked almost as young as Lily. Lily was beautiful in white.

I think most everyone in town had a hand in decorating the building we used for the dance. The colors used were red, white, and blue.

Everyone in the area was invited and the house was ready to party. In front of the band stand was a large dance area. The Grand March was so beautiful. They glided across the floor led by Missus Stuart and Mister Muller. Other town leaders followed. Lily invited a male friend to spend the first week in July at the Stuart farm. They were the very best looking young couple in the March. Father's partner was Missus Bell. Missus Bell's ball gown was black with a underskirt of scarlet. She looked so beautiful and was as good a dancer as anyone on the floor.

Now Father, of course, I thought no man could ever be as graceful or as handsome as he. Missus Bell had remodeled one of Mister Stuart's dress suits for him. He was to be her partner so she made sure that the suit fitted Father's body.

The band played well but with a restrained air as though they were in a class and had to read every note.

Father danced most of the numbers. He asked Missus Bell for the first dance. Otherwise, he was asked by the ladies of the town and was too much of a gentleman to refuse them. An hour into the evening, the music started for a dance that required a line of couples. Missus Stuart walked from about halfway across the room, her eyes never leaving my father's.

She held out her hand and said, "Alexander will you please dance the Virginia Reel with me?"

Father took her hand, gave a slight bow, then kissed her hand. Saying nothing, they took their place on the dance floor.

The set was a long one. After it was over, Father escorted Missus Stuart back to where Mister Stuart was standing, gave a short bow to the two of them and returned to stand with me.

Missus Stuart kept watching Father. I began to think he had done something of which she did not approve. Then Lily asked Father to dance. She was as graceful as a swan and Father's steps were tuned to hers at every turn.

When the music for the next Virginia Reel started, I saw Missus Stuart look over to where my father and I were standing. Father patted me on the head and started out the door.

I ran after him saying, "Missus Stuart wants to dance with you."

He kept right on walking. A number of men were outside and I knew the bottle they were passing to each other was not German wine.

Ole Joe called to him, "Mister Lamb, we were wondering when you would come out. Come, join us."

Father and the other men stayed outside until they heard a German yodel. The music had changed. The two German men were singing one of their country songs. Our farm hands thought they could yodel but the voices of these men had been trained in the Alp Mountains and their voice ranges were beyond belief. Without losing a beat, they went into an active dance, slapping their shoes and squatting on the floor—both in unison. This was all part of the plan for the gala.

The gala turned into a country song and dance. Ole Joe did an Irish jig. The Stonewall group sang two Scottish songs. Then there were three square dances. I was in a square with Rosa, Jed and Daniel. The Stuart group sang two songs with Missus Bell doing the solo part. Two farm hands from another area sang a ballad that made me want to cry about Mother, home, death and heaven.

The food, wine and punch had run out by that time and I guess we were all ready for home and bed. The last number was "The Star Spangled Banner," sung a'cappella by Missus Bell.

Success, success, success was the word I heard directed to Missus Stuart the next day. I even heard Father say to Missus Stuart,

"Your gala was planned so well, perhaps the Fourth of July should be celebrated with that much enthusiasm every year."

That must have been the longest sentence she ever heard Father speak.

Missus Stuart was so pleased and reached out as though to hug him. She was from Virginia. I have heard that people from the South do a lot of hugging. Instead of a hug, she caught his forearm in a tight grip. Mister Stuart walked up to them, greeted Father and the two men walked together toward the barn.

When I was very small Father would take my hands and whirl me round and round until he became dizzy. Sometimes he would stand behind me, put his arms under my shoulders, and do the same. Those times made me so happy that I continued whirling alone. After I got older, I wanted to whirl fast enough to take off into the air and fly like the angels. Rosa started whirling with me. We would do it for so long that sometimes we fell down laughing and giggling. One day that summer after falling in a fit of giggles, we looked up and saw Daniel standing over us. He was not sur-prised—he had seen us whirl lots of times.

This time Rosa saw over his shoulder, the tiny window in the attic of my house. Rosa said, "Cleo, what is in your attic?"

That led to Daniel getting a ladder from the barn and climb-ing onto the roof of the porch. With his pocket knife—all men and boys carried pocket knives—he forced open a built-in panel with the small window. The opening was about two feet square.

Daniel disappeared into the opening. "Go get me a lantern," he called.

We lit the lantern and passed it to him. Before he could hardly turn around, we were all three in that attic. The floor was just some rough boards laid across the beams to our great room. What a disappointment. All we saw was a small stack of short boards over to one side. We could tell that most of the house was made of logs. Inside and outside of the house had been covered over with lumber so no logs had been visible to us before. Daniel was interested in all this.

Rosa and I just wanted to get out of that dark place and into the sunlight. We remembered Missus Bell was making tea cakes—a small, sweet cookie—and we knew she would give us four each. She always limited us to four. We started towards the Stuarts' house whirling and dancing and giggling.

Daniel yelled to us to come back and help him. He had gathered up the pile of short boards, placed them on the porch roof and said, "Cleo, you and Rosa take these and lay them very carefully on the porch."

"Just throw them down on the ground and you pick them up later," Rosa answered.

"You do not know what I have found. Climb up the ladder, take them a board at a time, hand each board to Cleo. Cleo, you lay the boards flat in single file on the floor of the porch." He added, "Do not let the ends of them touch the dirt."

We did not always do what Daniel told us to do, but this time we started back. Father and Mister Stuart were near the barn and heard Daniel yelling. Daniel hardly ever raised his voice so they were sure something was wrong. They helped Daniel with the boards so Rosa and I left to get the cookies we were sure Missus Bell would give us.

Rosa said, "They are just dirty old boards. Daniel gets excited about stupid things."

After we ate our cookies, Rosa and I went back to see what had happened at our house.

Father said, "Cleo, you are going to get a hope chest."

I knew a "hope chest" was a trunk or chest a girl had to prepare for her married life. She was supposed to fill it with pretty things she had either made or had been given to her such as quilts, pillow cases, dishes, silver, things she could use in her new home. I said, "Those boards do not look like a chest to me."

Daniel said, "Come over here Cleo and let me show you the top of your chest."

The board he showed me was about forty inches long and

twenty-four inches wide. It had been wrapped in a piece of yel-lowed wool cloth. One side was partly carved with a tree stand-ing beside a flowing river.

Mister Stuart said, "I know this chest was cut out by either my great-grandfather or his brother, Daniel. The carving is similar to the small boxes in your extra bedroom. Those, we know, were carved by my great-uncle Daniel who died of pneumonia when he was about thirty. My guess is that this chest was to be a special gift for his mother and he did not live to finish it."

"We talked it over," said Daniel, "and your father is going to clean these boards and assemble a chest. I will finish what the other Daniel started. You will have a masterpiece."

Rosa could not sit still for that statement. "Brag, brag, brag. You think you are the best artist in the world." She stuck her tongue out at her brother.

Daniel ignored her.

For the next two weeks when Father was not doing farm work, most of his spare time was spent cleaning and polishing my "mas-terpiece."

"Oak, Cleo. This wood is oak." Father's eyes danced when he told me that.

It took Daniel more than two months to finish the carving the other Daniel had started. One Sunday late in the fall, he invited Father, the farm hands, Doctor Johnson, all the Stuarts, Missus Bell and Jed and I over for the unveiling of his masterpiece.

When I saw it, I cried. I recognized his inspiration at once. I had seen a drawing in one of Missus Stuart's art books of Cleopa-tra in her ship on the way to meet Marc Anthony. The big differ-ence was in Daniel's carving she was holding a lamb and there was a big tree in the foreground.

Ole Joe said, "Daniel carved about twenty lambs on other boards before he made a single knife mark on that top."

Missus Bell put both hands on her hips and declared, "Cleopa-tra MacRay Lamb, you have a masterpiece!"

The carving was put on the inside of the lid. Years later,

after Daniel Stuart became a world famous artist, this chest was searched for by every knowledgeable art collector in the world. It was known to exist. Little did the art world know it never left the Stuart farm.

The rest of that summer passed too quickly. It was the summer of my content. Nothing could go wrong. I had Father, a best friend in Rosa, my world seemed perfect. Sure we worked some. Missus Bell taught me how to sew, how to make patterns, how to tailor clothes. I loved it. Rosa hated sewing. When I sewed, she played the organ. I was good at what I did; she was pretty good at what she did. Missus Bell made school clothes for Jed and the Stuart children at home. I made my own clothes and made up my mind I would be the best dressed and smartest student in my school. Father and Missus Stuart helped me select books to study in any subject I was interested in. Science and theology were my favorites.

Chapter 4

*O*ne day toward the end of summer, the sun was shining, sky was clear, Father and Mister Stuart had gone away together on some farm business. They planned to return home before dark.

The feeling I had was not a vision but a sense of urgency. I felt compelled to gather everything in our garden. As fast as I could, I picked all the beans, peas, corn, tomatoes—even the little green ones. I stripped that garden, dug the beets and potatoes, picked turnip greens. I could not stop myself. Then I started on the apples, pears and grapes. James, the nosy brat, came over and saw what I was doing. He went home and told Missus Bell. Our great room was running over with all the things I had gathered. It was a warm day but I had built up a fire in the stove, gotten out our canning kettle and all the jars I could find. I was not as urged to can as I was to gather, but there was no way I was going to let that food spoil. Then I thought about my herb garden. After I had stripped the herbs, I started on flowers.

The garden was really a wreck by the time Rosa came over and said, "James told Missus Bell you had gone crazy. By the looks of this room, I think you have."

I started giggling. I too thought I must be crazy. It was too early in the year to gather most of those things, especially the ones that had not fully developed.

When Missus Bell asked us to do anything, we did it. Rosa said, "Missus Bell did not ask me to come get you. She ordered me to."

I went. When passing the Stuart's garden, I gathered up my apron and used it like a bag began to pick beans as fast as I could.

Rosa pulled my arm and said, "You are crazy. We only pick beans when we are asked to. Besides, Missus Bell is waiting."

Missus Bell took one look at me, sat down and gathered me in her arms. She said, "Cleo, Cleo, it is summer. You are loved. God has given us this beautiful day and he also has promised us tomorrow."

I cried and cried. Missus Bell held me while I sobbed. She did not mention what I had done but I knew she had been told.

When I was a little calmer, she said, "I will come over in a bit and help you with your canning. I will bring Jed and Daniel with me. They can help with lifting and maybe shuck the corn." She added, "Together we will get things taken care of."

Rosa put her arms around me and we went outside. "Let us do our whirl dance. We always have fun doing that."

Maybe I would have started to dance, except the air was so full of flying bugs they were getting in our hair, up our nose, even in our throats. Up higher, birds were flying south in such flocks you could hardly see the sun. Then came the bees flying to their hives as though they thought their Queen was in danger.

I said to Rosa, "Listen to the horses. I have never heard them make so much noise."

The cattle rushed to the south side of the fence. The fence went down almost at once. We could hear the roar of the cattle. That was the first time I ever saw a stampede. The sky became dark as we stood outside the kitchen. Small drops of rain fell. We were so amazed at how quickly our world had changed. We just stood there.

Then the hail started.

By the time we got back to the porch, Missus Stuart, Missus Bell, James, Annie Margaret and D.T. were there. I had heard of hail as big as goose eggs. This hail was only about the size of bird's eggs and the storm lasted only twenty minutes. The destruction it caused was unbelievable. Not only were the leaves gone from the trees, but limbs were broken. Glass in the windows on the north side of the Stuart house lay on the ground in a hundred pieces. The field of corn we could see from the porch was flattened. It took the farm hands days to fix the fences and round up the cattle. Later we found there had been quite a bit of damage done to the roof of the barn. I did not even look toward the Stuart's garden.

I was the first one to enter the Stuart house. Sitting in a chair by the kitchen stove minutes later, I watched everyone that had been on the porch come in. No one said a word. Missus Bell started breaking the beans I had picked. Missus Stuart took the two younger children with her to the front room of the house. James went to his room. Ole Joe came from the barn to see if everyone was all right. Rosa pulled a chair close to mine and took my hand.

D.T. came in from outside yelling, "Mother, Mother, Annie Margaret wants you!"

We all ran out to see what the fuss was about. Annie Margaret was squatting near an area we knew a mother hen had a nest with twelve eggs. We had been watching the nest for two weeks. James had found the nest and wanted to get the eggs. We talked him out of robbing the nest. It was late in the year for hens to hatch out little chicks but no one had told the hen that. You could hardly recognize that it was a hen. The hail had made her look like a mess of blood and feathers.

Annie Margaret said, "Get her off. Maybe the eggs are all right."

Missus Bell took a stick off the ground and pushed the carcass away. Underneath her, we found thirteen chicks, perfectly formed.

Rosa was the one that counted them, she counted them twice. "Where did the other chick come from? She only had twelve eggs."

Missus Bell answered. "One of her eggs had a double yolk and each yolk developed into a chick."

Annie Margaret started crying and that set the rest of us off.

35

Tears were in most everyone's eyes except James. James started laughing with joy. He said, "I knew that old hen was evil when I found her nest." He picked up the stick Missus Bell had dropped and started towards the chicks saying, "Those little chickens are evil, just like their mama. I am going to kill them."

Missus Bell caught him in a firm embrace and said, "James, you will not hurt those little chicks. God has spared them. I will not let you kill them."

Mister Stuart and Daniel heard the noise we were making and came to see what was wrong. Mister Stuart took a look at the situation and told Daniel to go to the barn, get a box and a small horse blanket. Mister Stuart said, "We cannot watch James every minute. These chicks will never be safe from him."

The adults talked it over and decided that Daniel should take the chicks to the Stonewalls.

"Missus Stonewall would know how to care for them," Missus Bell said.

The three of us, Missus Bell, Rosa and I, stayed in the kitchen until Mister Stuart and Father came home. Missus Bell met them on the porch. They talked a few minutes then Father came in, took my hand and said, "Come, Cleo."

The hail was so deep we had to push it aside to walk home. It was not really late—it was not even dark. I was so tired I went over to my bunk bed, laid on my side with my back to the room. Father kissed the top of my head. I went to sleep. Three hours later I woke, turned over and saw Father reading by lamp light. He smiled at me, put down his book, went over to the stove and filled a bowl with soup. He said, "Come and eat."

That soup was made with some of the vegetables I had gathered earlier in the day. It had just the right amount of butter and milk added. I started laughing and giggling and talking about the hail storm. I talked about the horses, cows, birds, insects, corn, the Stuarts' garden, but I said nothing about our garden. We were almost covered over with the produce I had gathered. I talked about Ole Joe coming to check on us after the storm. Never did I call him "Ole Joe." I always said,"Mister Ole Joe."

Father had put his book down and gave me his full attention. Father was always careful with any book he ever touched. He also taught me to treat books the same way.

The next morning Missus Stuart, Missus Bell, Rosa and the two little Stuarts came over with extra jars, sugar, salt and vinegar to help me preserve what I had gathered the day before. All the men and boys were out trying to bring some order to the damage done by the hail storm. The women, Rosa and I had worked together before and knew each other's strong points. Missus Bell took charge and we worked steady. We even cooked potatoes in the backyard in an iron pot which was usually used for washing. When we had finished cooking potatoes, we put in the beans. Some of the potatoes were no bigger than the hail stones that fell the day before.

Rosa and I chattered the whole time, but worked hard. The chicken experience put a damper on our day. Rosa told about what Mister Stuart and Father had heard the day before when they were in town. Two farm hands from the Stonewall farm had been caught out on the range. Their horses had run away and one of the boys was killed. The one that lived saved himself by hugging tight to an oak tree.

He later said he heard the tree say, "come."

When I heard this, I smiled and thought, So trees do talk. I am not the only one that hears them.

Daniel and Jed had been in the north section of the Stuart farm before the storm. They had finished mending the fence, fed their horses and gone into one of the farm shacks to eat their lunch. After eating, Jed read. Daniel carved on a piece of wood that was beginning to look like a lamb. They heard the horses screaming. When they went outside, the horses were excited and trying to get out of the lot. Each boy went to his horse to calm it and lead it back under the shelter. Then the darkness came and the hail fell. During the storm itself, the horses stood still but their bodies quivered. Daniel and Jed told us later that their bodies were quivering also.

Every person on the Stuart farm made it through the storm safely. We lost some animals and some buildings were damaged. The crops were all gone—there was nothing left in the garden. The following winter, Mister Stuart had to buy food for everything he had to feed on that farm including his family. The Stuarts were lucky. They had a lot of income from the coal mines in Virginia. Most of the other farmers were not that lucky. I know Mister Stuart's money helped many of his neighbors get through the next winter.

Our lives gradually went back to normal. There was not as much outside work for Rosa and me to do, so we had a good time riding horses and taking the buggy to town, shopping and visiting friends. We were always trying to get away from James, as he was always trying to be just where we were. We still danced and whirled when we could. I talked, Rosa giggled. The only thing that was never talked about by me or anyone else in my presence was how I knew to gather the things from our garden before the hail storm.

Annie Margaret did say, "Cleo, why did you go crazy the other day?"

I did not have to answer her because Rosa pushed her to the ground, stood over her and said, "Shut up Annie Margaret or I will tell Father on you."

I was glad I did not have to answer her question, for I had no answer. I did not know what caused me to strip our garden and fruit trees.

Chapter 5

*S*ummer stayed with us until winter came—there seemed to be no autumn. Oh yes, the leaves turned red, yellow, orange—you pick a color, it was there. But the grass was still green and the horses, cows, sheep, hogs, chickens and people stayed outside enjoying the mild weather until a day late in October. Someone must have left the north gate open for cold whipped in from the north. You could just see the gods of the winds all blowing at once. Jack Frost painted the windows and turned the green grass to mush. It was no surprise. We were ready for winter.

Winter gave us time for reading, visiting, sleeping. Friday started sleeping again in her bed behind the stove when she was not curled up in Father's lap. My lap moved around too much for her to get comfortable. There was always plenty to read. Missus Stuart ordered books once a month from New York, some even in Latin, French or Greek. She was always amazed at the extent of my father's knowledge. I think she was even a little in love with him, although I was so enamored with him I was sure everyone else loved him, too.

On that first cold winter day, Father was out doing barn work. I was drawn to the room behind the fireplace. We had not needed it and had decided not to disturb the ghost of the little old woman we thought haunted the room.

Very seldom had I asked my psychic powers to work for me. After my visions my head would hurt or my stomach ached, always I became sleepy. This time I was determined to try to help the ghost in the best bedroom in our house to go on to the next level of her spiritual life.

How long ago the logs in that little fireplace had been laid I did not know. They were really dry and started burning as soon as I brought a start of fire from the stove and touched them with it. I said to the lady in the picture, "I have come to visit. I know you will not be serving me tea and really chat with me. So I am going to get warm and comfortable."

With that, I took off my shoes, pulled down the blue and white coverlet as well as the two quilts, arranged the pillow and lay down on the yellow homespun sheet. I was ready to meet the ghost and hear her story.

Friday slunk through the open door—that should have told me something. With a small "meow," she leaped on the bed and got comfortable curled around my head. We all know how sensitive cats are to spirits. She was purring in two seconds. I waited. No vision came to me. What woke me was Friday jumping off the bed and the sound of Father putting wood in the stove.

Entering the great room, I spilled out my story of the ghost no show. I was just as enthused about not seeing the old lady that I thought haunted the bedroom as I would have been if she had appeared. Together we decided to invite Mister and Missus Stuart over that evening and solve the mystery of the closed door.

This was the first formal invitation we had ever given to anyone to visit us. Yes, I know "formal" means cards, dress up and drinks. I guess I mean it was the first time we had invited someone to come at a certain time.

Mister and Missus Stuart knocked on the door just as we expected. After we talked about the weather, cows, hog killing and Missus Bell's niece coming to visit, we ate our cookies and drank our coffees. Much as I like to talk, I thought we were wasting time, so right in the middle of talk about how cold the winters were when Mister Stuart was a boy, I got up, opened the door to the mystery bedroom and said, "Please explain about this room."

The room became quiet. Both Mister and Missus Stuart sat

very still. Then, as though on cue, both stood, and walked together into the mystery room. Without speaking or touching anything, they looked around as though they had not seen it before.

After what seemed to me an hour but was only a few minutes, they returned to their chairs and Mister Stuart told us the story of his grandfather.

Mister Stuart said that Alexander Stuart left Scotland for America when he was thirty years old. He left his mother and two sisters in Glasgow. His younger brother Daniel came with him. Somehow, Mister Stuart was not sure how, maybe he bought it or maybe it was a grant, he and his brother acquired over two thousand acres in this land of Indiana. Working hard and with the help of neighbors, they cleared land, built a log cabin, and established a farm. Their plan was to send for their mother. Into this cabin, they built the "mystery room." The picture on the wall was not their mother. It was a picture they saw in a store window that reminded them of her. The boxes were carved by Daniel. The chest was made by Alexander.

It took them five years before they were ready to send for their mother. Five years is a long time, many things can happen. One evening Daniel came home from trapping, cold, wet and shivering. His lungs filled with fluid, breathing became difficult. None of the things Alexander or his neighbors did for him had helped, mustard plasters, boiled onions, hot bricks. In three days, he was dead. At thirty-one years, fifty-three days, a strong man was put into his grave.

When their mother in Scotland got the news of this death, she just gave up. She had not told Alexander of her declining health. His prayer had been that he would soon see her. That was not to be. She died a month later. Her room in Indiana was never used by her.

After a period of mourning, Alexander married a young woman from two farms over. Except for cleaning, he did not want his mother's bedroom disturbed. Had he and his wife had a bunch of children, things might have been different. They had only one child, Daniel. Mister Stuart said that his father Daniel claimed that as a child he would sneak into the closed "Granny room" once in a while, always careful to close the door.

Somehow when he was about eight, he went to sleep under the bed. Clumsy hands yanked him out, scraping his face against the ropes and waking him. The leather belt was used on his back side. His mother then gave him a "talking to." She explained to him that his father's anger was not due to him being in the closed room. It was due to them not being able to find him for five hours. Everyone, neighbors and farm hands had looked for him. Mister Stuart's father said he never even touched the door of Granny's room again.

Mister Stuart said his grandparents made good farmers. America was coming awake. He raised beef cattle, corn, and other crops to sustain his family and workers. Prosperous beyond his belief, they went south in the early spring to buy calves, then drove them to this farm. The calves ate and grew bigger on the grass that grew in such abundance in this rich, rich new land. After frost came, he and his men rounded the calves up and drove them to the stockyards outside of Chicago. It was a good life and there were always plenty of boys that knew horses and wanted a job to help with the farm. Some of them later went west and became "ranchers." Mister Stuart said, "We always called ourselves 'farmers.'"

Mister Stuart's father was about twenty years old when a beautiful girl, Ruth Franklin from southern Virginia, came to visit Doctor Johnson, the father of the present Doctor Johnson. They met by chance on the main street in Arcidia. Both were smitten. A year later they were married. Together they planned the house the Stuarts live in today. Two stories, six rooms. Later they added the back addition and later still Mister Stuart added three rooms off that.

His mother's family in Virginia owned quite a bit of land that did not look like much and was almost impossible to farm. Just under the surface was the blackest coal known to man. They received enough money from those mines to keep all the family happy and the farm going, if he never sold another pound of beef. That was not going to happen. He loved what he did and wanted his grandchildren to grow up on this farm. His parents planned a large family. He arrived after they were married two years. Then no more children and no miscarriages, just him.

His thoughts returned to the mystery room. His grandmother kept it clean but unused as his grandfather requested. Word got around that the room was haunted. People said they saw curtains move, a light or a face in the window, heard moans, even said the walls under the window glowed with a fiery, white light. His family did not start these rumors or add to them. They were amused by the stories that got back to them.

After his grandparents died, they began using this house for their married hired hands and families. They had all heard of the ghost room and did not use it, would not even enter it. It became a well-kept family joke. The family's housekeeper would come over every two weeks to clean and dust everything. Twice a year was a spring and Christmas general cleaning. Washing the curtains, airing the covers, tightening the ropes on the bed if needed, taking the wood from the fireplace and dusting there. Putting new wood back in.

Missus Stuart said, "Missus Bell does this still. It is a way to inspect the house. The families that have lived here have been good housekeepers because of this. We were surprised when you did not use the room for we knew you had not heard our family ghost story. We just kept quiet. Please use the room. It is neither a shrine or haunted."

Even though we had to keep more wood in the stove to heat more space, we never again closed the "Granny room" door.

Mary Lee, Missus Bell's niece, came the next day. Her husband was so handsome. They had been married seven months but he treated her as if they were still on their honeymoon. The plan was for Mary Lee to stay at the farm with Missus Bell while her husband went to Chicago with Father and Mister Stuart. Missus

Bell always stayed with me when Father was gone overnight, so it was decided, instead, that Mary Lee would sleep over with me.

Talk? I thought I was a talker, but that girl could talk the legs off a June bug. As soon as she removed her coat, I knew there would be another member of her family soon. I heard all—well, almost all—about her courtship, wedding, lovemaking. She seemed to forget I was ten years old, and eager to learn.

I talked just enough to keep her going. She had me feel her stomach and the baby was kicking so often I moved my chair closer and kept my right hand on her stomach. In two months, she said her baby would be in her arms and drinking from her breast.

She was so much in love and happy about her baby and said you had to be married over nine months to have a baby and she had only been married seven months. It was very late when we went to bed.

The dried raspberry leaves I brewed and sweetened with honey had tasted good and kept our mouths from being dry from talking. I knew raspberry tea was good for women and especially good for women great with child and she was both.

We slept late the next morning, saw no one else until midmorning and said goodbye to Missus Stuart and Missus Bell as they left to go to Arcidia. They did this every third Saturday of the month. After lunch, they cleaned and put flowers in the church, then felt free to visit and shop. They always went alone; they called it their "party day."

I know for sure it was not all party. Their visits were often to call on patients of Doctor Johnson. Sometimes Missus Stuart did things for those people she never did at home, like cleaning windows and changing beds. Once she canned twenty-four cans of tomatoes while Missus Bell sat by the bed and read the Bible to a lady who was spending her last day on earth. Except for lunch and shopping, I never did figure out the fun part.

Mary Lee and I had lunch, then decided on a long walk. She wanted to see where we did our swimming in the summer. She told me, again, about how warm her husband's back had been the day before when she rode behind him on their beautiful horse. Her man, her house, her baby, her everything—entering her world was what I wanted to do.

We did not get to the river, instead the river came to us. Well, almost. Water started running from her body, even wetting the skirt she was wearing. During our walk, she had stopped several times, her eyes getting real wide. I thought that baby is really kicking. She even doubled over once.

When her water broke, I knew that baby was not just kicking but on his way out. We started back to the house slowly. Her pains were regular and intense. The door to Granny's room was the first thing that caught my attention. As we entered the house, it seemed to invite us in. Removing her soiled clothes took us quite a spell. I tried to keep my eyes closed but she had so many petticoats on I had to open them to untie the strings. She had packed three nightgowns. I took the oldest-looking one out of the carpet bag she had brought with her. I was trying to help her put it on when she had a contraction I could not believe she would live through.

While she walked back and forth, I made up a pad with about ten layers of newspaper covered with part of an old sheet. I had seen too many animal births, and heard too many women talk not to believe there would be blood involved.

I completely removed the cover and two quilts from the bed, put the pad I had made across three-quarters of the bed and helped Mary Lee to lie down. Somehow I kept her talking until her next contraction.

I said, "Mary Lee, when the next pain starts, you may hold my hands and that may help."

Believe me, that was the wrong move. If I had not been able to get my hands away from her, they would have been crushed. Another mistake I made was to light that fire in the fireplace. By the time that baby came, we were both wet with sweat.

I had been told this was a premature baby. Having heard stories of tiny babies being wrapped in warm blankets and put into an open warm oven, I let the fire in the fireplace get low and put a soft towel in the fireplace oven to get warm. Rolling another towel and tying it with a rope, I told Mary Lee to pull on that. I tied the two ends of the rope to the head bed posts.

No way was I going to let her get hold of my hands again. I covered her with a quilt from my bunk bed.

Between contractions I put two metal buckets of water on the stove, and got out my father's largest medical book to read up on births. It was really just a review, as there had been nothing I had ever been curious about that he had not explained.

Somehow Mary Lee and I got through the next two hours. When I saw that large spot of black hair, I knew that baby was ready to meet the world. What a large premature baby! He was crying by the time he was out of that tunnel. A little mess was on my hurriedly constructed pad but not much blood. I just cleaned his eyes—his yelling told me his mouth was clear. I wrapped him in the soft towel I had heated in the fireplace oven to prepare for a tiny baby.

This boy was not tiny and he was hungry. I lay the yelling boy on Mary Lee's chest and massaged her stomach to help her get rid of the afterbirth. She exposed her breast as if the feeding of a baby had been something she had experienced before. The baby took two sucks and was asleep. Mary Lee was asleep before I could get her and the bed cleaned up.

I was so tired I was shaking, but so pleased with myself I was giddy. Determined that everything would be in order when Missus Stuart and Missus Bell got back from their trip to town, I kept working. Washing Mary Lee's clothes, putting the two quilts and blue and white cover on the new mother and child, wrapping the soiled pad and afterbirth in newspaper. I considered burning or burying it but changed my mind. The medical book did not tell me how to dispose of it.

What to do with the two buckets of boiling water was a mystery to me. All they did was steam up the great room. They were too heavy and too hot for me to move. I left them boiling away. Since that time, I have come to realize Mary Lee had an easy time. Just three hours of labor with her first baby.

Missus Stuart and Missus Bell drove their buggy first to the Stuart house and a farm boy unloaded the things they brought and drove the buggy to the barn. Then the two ladies walked over to our house. I met them on the porch. My eyes and smile must have startled them for they both asked at once, "Where is Mary Lee?"

I tried to be casual so I said, "Oh, she is in Granny's room."

The room she had been sleeping in was the one with two single beds. So I knew the women would wonder why she had moved to Granny's room. Up until that time, no one had spent the night in Granny's room.

I opened the front door; Missus Stuart went in, then Missus Bell. I followed.

The ladies both asked at once, "Why do you have the house so hot?"

Missus Bell said, "This room is really steamy."

Putting my finger up to my mouth in the "be quiet" gesture, I pointed toward the open door of Granny's room. Missus Bell entered the room first. Even I was impressed by the scene of the sleeping mother and babe. We all three backed out of the room and whispered as though we were in church.

My story amazed them. Missus Bell was very interested in the medical book I had used—that I had tied and cut the cord as instructed, even putting a binding around the belly of the baby.

We must have made more noise than we thought for in about a half hour Mary Lee called out for me.

After that Missus Bell took over. She fixed a bed for the baby in a dresser drawer. Bathed the baby—it was covered with white flakes—changed the makeshift diaper I had put on it. I am glad she did. What was in the diaper looked black and sticky but, surprisingly, had no odor. I would have been sure something was wrong had I changed it. We were all so excited when that little guy started to take his first breast milk. Mary Lee could not explain the burst of passion she felt as her milk began to flow.

It was arranged that Missus Bell would sleep in my bunk bed to be closer to Granny's room in case Mary Lee or the baby needed anything during the night. I slept in the bed Mary Lee had used the night before. I was so tired I knew nothing would keep me from sleeping for the next twelve hours. But only a little while later I heard sounds that that little house had never heard before. Missus Bell and Mary Lee were singing. Singing like I had never heard before. Later we heard that the four farm hands from the bunk house had heard them and had been sitting on the porch of our house, listening.

Chapter 6

*N*eedless to say, I joined the two women. I did not sing, I just enjoyed their singing. This went on about two hours. It turned out that Missus Bell's father—Mary Lee's grandfather—was a singing teacher from Wales. They grew up singing harmony, learning the old Welsh songs as well as new songs and hymns from many different religions. That little baby was full of his mother's milk and slept through the whole thing.

What Missus Bell told Mary Lee about conception, I do not know, but I am sure Mary Lee was told that walking down the aisle and having a preacher say a few words is not how a baby is started and that a healthy seven-pound-nine-ounce boy is not premature.

Three days later the three men who went to Chicago, Mister Stuart, Father and Richard—Mary Lee's husband—returned. Richard was real pleased with his new baby but to my sharp eyes it was evident that he was not really surprised. He could count back nine months and remember. Two days later one of the farm hands rode Richard's horse and the new father, mother and baby went home, in style, driving Mister Stuart's best buggy. That was the last time I saw them. Just after Christmas, they moved out west to work on a cattle ranch. Talking to the owner of the ranch had been Richard's reason for going to Chicago.

Missus Bell told me they named the baby Richard Evans Poe. Evans was Mary Lee and Missus Bell's maiden name. He may have been named Richard but to me he was always "number one"—the very first baby I helped a mother deliver.

By then the Stuarts, the Bells, the farm hands, a group of neighbor men and the veterinarian heard my story. For the next week, I was a "little mom." I talked and talked about my three hours with Mary Lee and little Richard. As usual after I quit talking, the farm hands forgot I was there and began telling stories of births they had seen or heard. One man said his neighbor's baby would not nurse and the mother was afraid of developing cake breast or milk fever so sometimes she put a puppy or kitten to her breast to drink her milk and relieve the pressure. When the circus was in town five years ago, the veterinarian said he was called to a tent when a circus woman was having a baby. When he asked her who the father of her baby was, she replied, "If you stuck your finger in a buzz saw, would you know which tooth bit you?" That got a big laugh.

Chapter 7

I wish my second sight had been working since vision would have been a forewarning. In early November Missus Stuart's Uncle Frank came to visit. When he was young he must have been almost as handsome as Father. Now he was a little gray and a bit overweight. His voice and laugh were nice to hear. I liked and trusted him at once. The three men, Father, Mister Stuart and Uncle Frank, spent a lot of time together both in Mister Stuart's office and standing together outside. Later Missus Stuart was included in their conversation.

No, a vision did not come to me, but I knew Father and I would be moving on. The beef cattle had already been driven to Chicago. Winter was at hand and Father seemed ready for a change. What surprised me was where we were going. Uncle Frank was a steamship captain on the Mississippi River and he wanted someone to run a new business he was starting. This new business had to do with barges. Father had always loved being around water and was a good man to lead men. Money had never been very important to Father, but Uncle Frank offered him more money, a house, personal insurance, good schools for me and hinted of a more advanced social life for Father. Uncle Frank was a bachelor and liked the ladies. Father was a healthy man, thirty years old and, to me, the most beautiful man on earth. He had the shoulders of a swimmer and the long legs of a cowboy. Besides that, the power of his brain was more than could be measured.

The surprise for me was that I would not be going with him. It was arranged for me to move in with the Stuarts until the end of the school year. Father would go to Mississippi with Uncle Frank. When he returned in the spring, we would pack our wagon and really move to the banks of that big, big river called "the Mississippi." Until then, I was unhappy in a large way for I felt I would lose my soul mate, Rosa. The Bells and the Stuarts had also become important to me and Missus Stuart was trying so hard to turn me into a "lady." Rosa was my very best friend, the only "best friend" I had ever had.

Saying goodbye to Father was a few tears, many hugs, fifty-seven kisses but really not too bad. Ten minutes later Rosa and I were giggling about maybe sometime kissing boys that many times.

I talked and read anything I could about Mississippi. I studied the river, the towns, the ships, the barges. Once a week I received a letter from Father. He talked about his "our" house, his job, the people he worked with. He never had been much of a talker but wrote long, interesting letters. These were the first and only letters I ever received from him. In the last letter he told me he had bought my Christmas present and would be sending it soon. He also told me how much he loved me and how much he missed me.

During the second week in December, Rosa and I looked out the window and saw a strange man riding up the lane really fast. The man and horse looked as though they had been riding long and hard. I heard Missus Bell answer the door and take the stranger into Mister Stuart's office.

Rosa and I ran into the office because we did not want to miss anything. We heard the man say, "Mister Alexander Lamb has been decapitated."

The man handed Mister Stuart a large tan envelope. I watched Mister Stuart take it and turn pale. I stood very still. My spine reacted to the news of my father's death before my brain. The nerves at the bottom of my spine pounded with pain that slowly traveled all the way to my brain. The message was, "Your father is dead."

I could not move. I sensed Missus Stuart's presence before feeling her hands on my shoulders. From behind she hugged me close. Rosa and Missus Bell sobbed. Otherwise, everyone in the room was still.

Time passed, I am not sure how much later it was when I heard Missus Stuart say, "Missus Bell, please see to the comfort of this gentleman. He needs a bath, some food and a bed. Let him sleep in the bedroom across from Daniel's room."

My memory of the next hours is vague. I know Doctor Johnson was sent for and I remember drinking a liquid he gave me.

I awoke to hear Missus Bell say to Missus Stuart, "The man from Mississippi has been cared for and is asleep. He said he did not know what decapitated meant until Mister Frank told him it meant Mister Lamb's head had been cut off." Missus Bell continued, "He used the word 'decapitated' about twenty times while he was eating his meal. He appeared very tired and not aware of what he was saying."

That was all I heard. Sleep overcame me, again. The next thing I knew it was about ten o'clock the next day. Missus Bell sat in a chair by the window in my room. A pillowcase she had been embroidering was in her lap, but she was not working on it. She was just looking out the window and crying.

Missus Bell did not see me get out of bed. Nor was she aware that I was no longer asleep until I was right beside her. I knelt and put my head in her lap. She put her arms around my head and sobbed. I did not cry and was unable to speak. After a few minutes I got up, went to the dresser, got my hair brush, and brushed my hair. Then I got dressed in the same clothes I had worn the day before.

Was Doctor Johnson wrong to use drugs to help me get through the early time of my grief? Right or wrong, that is what he did, and we can never undo what has already happened. Most of us do what we think best at the moment, and I am sure that is what the doctor did.

That is also what my father did when he stepped into the Mississippi to try to save the fifteen-year-old boy called Slim. Slim had been knocked off the barge on which he and my father were working. A barrel got loose while Slim's back was turned. It hit him; he lost his balance and landed in the river. My father knew Slim could not swim, for they had talked earlier in the day about finding a shallow place in the river, so Father could teach him. It must have seemed so simple to Father to step off the barge and pull Slim out.

What can I say? I survived. My life changed. My appetite for food diminished, my hair was often a tangled mess. Some nights I slept in the clothes I had worn all day, moving slowly, sitting for hours at a time, my hands in my lap. Maybe holding a book or a bit of embroidery, just holding it, not reading or using a needle. Talking was something I seemed to have forgotten how to do. I still said things like "thank you" and "please." My desire was to become invisible. If Missus Bell or Missus Stuart asked me to do something, I did it, just that, no more. Even though I was there in person, my spirit had retreated somewhere inside of me.

The Stuart family was also subdued. Annie Margaret, five, and David Thomas, three, were the only ones who did not seem affected. They could not understand all the changes that took place around them.

Two boxes arrived from Mississippi addressed to me. My Christmas present from Father was carefully wrapped in heavy brown paper. The package contained six yards of emerald green silk with a white interwoven border of the Greek Key. My favorite color trimmed with my favorite emblem. Father had selected my gift with great care.

The other box sent by Uncle Frank was a trunk—the same trunk Father had taken with him to Mississippi. Among other things contained his saddle, a horse blanket, his boots, a few pieces of clothing, writing material, and a sketch Daniel had made of me and given him as he was leaving with Uncle Frank. There was also a chess set I had insisted Father take with him. The set had a marble board with the chess pieces carved in marble in the shapes of Greek gods and goddesses. This set had been given to him when he was ten years old by the two Greek nuns that had taken care of him from age two until sixteen. The many letters I had written Father since he left for Mississippi were also in the trunk. Two were still unopened. I wrapped the silk material carefully and put it in the bottom of the chest that Father and Daniel had made for me. I closed Father's trunk and did not cry.

Christmas that year of eighteen hundred and fifty-eight was celebrated by the Stuarts with the same food, visits, guests, gifts and parties they always enjoyed. I went through the Christmas season in a daze, helped Missus Bell some, Missus Stuart some. I talked sparingly and stayed in my room through most of the time. Friday seemed to sense my despair. She tried to get my mood to lift by sitting on my lap, sometimes brushing against my feet. I would push her off. I did not even notice when she was not around. Father and I had always been careful not to let her outside alone. We did not want her to have kittens, and there were three Tom cats that stayed around the barn and bunk house. Ole Joe could make two of them jump three feet in the air. Twice a day he would shoot milk towards them as he milked the cows.

With the start of the New Year of eighteen hundred and fifty-nine, my mood became darker. I wrote angry letters, none of which I mailed. I blamed the death of my father on everyone. The first of these letters I wrote to Missus Stuart after seeing her crying in the kitchen with Missus Bell. I heard her say to Missus Bell, "Alexander would not have gone to Mississippi if I had not been drawn to him."

Missus Bell took her hands and said, "Grace, do not blame yourself."

Missus Stuart replied, "When I was near him, I could not keep from flirting with him, even touching him though he never encouraged me. The only time he ever touched me was when I asked him to dance with me at the gala last Fourth of July."

Anguish caused by my father's death was destroying me. Anguish drove my thoughts and actions. In my heart I knew Missus Stuart was not to blame. I could have told her Father was always moving on, that women were constantly drawn to him. I could have told her before we moved to our cave last fall, the daughter of a shopkeeper had decided he was going to be her husband. Even that was not the reason for our move. Father just wanted to be someplace else and I was happy to be wherever he was.

Other hateful, angry letters I wrote to Uncle Frank, Mister Muller, the German man who helped Missus Stuart organize the Gala, the man from Mississippi who brought the message of Father's death. Then I started on Jesus, Apollo, Buddha, and the Oak Tree. The Oak Tree letter was the only one I tried to deliver. Our oak in the wood near which we built the magic circle did not have knot holes. So I found an oak nearby with a knothole and packed my letter addressed to the "God of the Oak" in it.

One letter I did not put on paper but formed in my mind was to "God of the Universe." Somehow I could not blame God for my father's death although I think He was the real guilty one. Perhaps Father was not running away from but running toward his destiny. Father knew the Stuarts would give me a safe and secure home, better than he had been able to provide. No, I do not think God planned Father's death. I do think it was God's will that he would die in that muddy water. I hid the other angry letters in the bottom of Father's trunk.

We went back to school in early January. The classroom was the same, the teacher was the same. I was different. I did my assigned work, but I was no longer a "challenge." No longer did I try to outsmart everyone else, including my teacher—no longer did I talk unless it was absolutely necessary. My appearance changed. My hair was unkempt. My dress was sometimes a little dirty and wrinkled. A few times I forgot my belt. Rosa began to notice when the other students started teasing me about my disheveled appearance.

After about a week Missus Bell started checking "her girls" before we left for school. She spent as much time checking Rosa as she did me, pretending that Rosa was as careless as I. She would brush her hair a little, pat her dress. When she came to me there was a real inspection which always resulted in a hair brushing. Once she pulled my dress over my head and said, "I forgot to wash this dress. I cannot have you looking like a ragamuffin." I had to rush back to my room in my underclothes to get another dress. After that I was more careful with my appearance.

In the classroom and on the playground, I retreated into my shell. Soon most of the students forgot about me. I went from being the most attention-hungry person to an almost invisible clump. Often I heard the word "decapitated" as the students practiced a new word.

January, February, and March passed. Rosa started spending more time with other girls, often three or four were gathered around her at school and they also began coming to the farm. I would drift away, sometimes riding my horse with the hired hands as they tended the beef cattle or fences. If I went off alone, someone would follow me. Ole Joe, James, Jed but most often it was Daniel. I am not sure what the Stuarts thought I might do or where I might go, but they wanted me to know I was not alone. I could see them—they were not trying to hide. I had the feeling they just wanted me to know they were there if I needed them. Ole Joe always had his knife and something to whittle with him. James' passion was rocks. He spent a lot of time throwing rocks. He was nine years old, and boys like to throw things. Jed took a book with him, always reading about farms, ranches or stations which he said was what cattle people in Australia called their cattle farms. Always the artist, Daniel had his sketch paper. Even his Bible had tiny sketches all through it.

During this period I had many visions. Once I "saw" four people in a buggy with a runaway horse coming down a very steep road on a mountain. Two men and two women terrified, the horse going at break-neck speed took himself, the buggy and the four people off a steep bank into a very deep lake. I watched as all the people and the horse drowned. The lake was so deep none of them ever came up for air. They became one of the mysteries you read about. It was said "they disappeared in thin air." To whom or where this happened was never revealed to me. I also "saw" a beautiful woman, a man, and a driver killed in a tunnel. I heard the crash and smelled the smoke. Also I saw many shipwrecks. Some I had seen in my visions before.

One vision I had was of a young man being knocked off a barge by a loose barrel. He was already in the water before I realized that it was Slim. Slim did not panic, he knew he would be saved by Mister Lamb. Slim heard my father step into the water from the barge. Father did not dive, he went in feet first. Father saw Slim come up to the water surface, take a breath and sink again. Father then slipped into the muddy water trying to locate Slim. As Father came up for air, he was not aware of the chain until it was around his neck. One end of the chain had come loose from the barge and formed a loop. His hands went up to his throat just as a heavy log hit the cable. I saw his head become completely severed. His head landed on the barge.There was very little blood, his heart quit beating almost at once. No message was sent by the nerves in his brain to his heart to pump blood. His body remained tangled in the chain that killed him.

Slim's head surfaced. I heard him say, "My name is Robert Durwood Spencer," before sinking into the waters of the Mississippi river.

In my vision, I saw the look of shock on the men's faces as they stood on the barge. They had been sure Slim's rescue would be simple. People often fell off barges, few ever drowned. When they realized Father's head was severed from his body, they, too, tried to rescue Slim. It was too late. Both bodies were soon on the barge. Bad news traveled fast. By the time the barge made shore, Uncle Frank was there to meet it. The first thing I did when the vision was over was to write "Robert Durwood Spencer" on my writing pad. I knew Slim did not want "name unknown" on his

58

grave stone.

After this vision I was really sick, my stomach must have turned over. The vomiting and diarrhea were intense. All my visions had some effect on my body, but none had been as severe as this one. When there was nothing left in my stomach, I fell asleep. This was Sunday night or Monday morning about two o 'clock. Just after seven on Monday morning, I felt Missus Bell shaking me. It was a school day and the family was always downstairs for breakfast by seven o 'clock.

I said, "Missus Bell, please not today."

She let me sleep. Friday woke me by trying to give me a bath. She licked the salt off my cheeks. I do not remember crying, but the salt must have come from my tears.

Uncle Frank wrote Mister Stuart and asked him to ask me to help him design Father's grave marker. I wanted a lamb in a resting position carved on top of a round top marble stone, the word "Father" straight across. Underneath this, the word "Peace." Then Father's name, Alexander Lee Lamb, born Isle of Bute, Scotland, May 10, 1828, Died December 18, 1858. Below that the engraved image of a large tree, just trunk and limbs, no leaves. Daniel drew the sketch I sent to Uncle Frank.

Annie Margaret said, "That looks just like the baby headstones in the cemetery we play in every Sunday behind church." She added, "They have lambs just like that on top of them." She had always addressed my father as Mister Lamb but did not associate the name Lamb with a baby sheep.

I wrote to Uncle Frank that I appreciated him sending Father's trunk. I also mentioned, "Father wrote me a lot about the area in which he was working and about the people he worked with. Slim's name is Robert Durwood Spencer. I do not know his exact age but I think he was about fifteen."

I did not discuss my visions with anyone. Somehow I was sure Slim wanted his real name on his tombstone and Uncle Frank had written he was having a stone made that said "Slim" and "Died by drowning December 18, 1858." I knew the way my letter was worded to Uncle Frank he would think Father had written Slim's real name to me.

Toward the last of March, I went to my room and found Friday in the middle of my bed with four newborn kittens, one black, two black and white, and one little grey runt. They were all getting their dinner. Friday looked so proud. This scene made me feel like a complete failure. My whole life had gone to pieces. I could not even protect a cat.

Doctor Johnson was a personal friend of the Stuarts and came over often to visit. He tried hard to help me get over my depression. He gave me pills that I accepted but did not take and told Missus Bell about food that should help me. I ate very little.

The evening of the day Friday had her kittens, I was waiting for him. I had Friday and her kittens in a box and said to Doctor Johnson, "I am a failure. I don't want this ugly cat family around me. If you don't take them, I am going to ask James to kill them."

James, along with me, had started to do strange things. He beat to death a setting hen. When asked why, he said, "It's that old hen's fault that the hail came and destroyed everything." He did not remember that the hen he had been angry about had died in the hail storm.

When I handed Doctor Johnson the box of cats, he said, "Cleo, maybe I cannot help you get over your grief, I cannot bring back your father, but I can find a good home for Friday and her kittens."

That was the last time I saw Friday, who was the only personal pet I ever had.

Chapter 8

*A*pril first, eighteen-fifty-nine was a dark and dreary day. There was no school. Maybe it was a Saturday. Nothing I did seemed right. I could not get the covers on my bed straight. I spilled my milk at breakfast and almost fell as I stepped off the kitchen porch steps. Even my horse treated me like a stranger. As I rode out of the horse barn lot, I saw Daniel putting a saddle on his horse. I rode slowly, I had learned there was no way I could escape the eyes of the Stuarts. After Daniel was ready to ride, I kicked my horse to a run.

Riding as fast as possible towards the north end of the farm and knowing most of the cows would be there, my plan was to ride that horse straight into two hundred and fifty cattle. What happened to me, my horse, nor the cattle was not on my mind. There had to be a change in my life and I did not know how to make it happen.

Daniel's horse was bigger and faster than mine. He cut in front of me and turned my horse about one hundred yards from the cows I was aiming toward. Catching the bridle of my horse, he rode beside us until we slowly came to a stop.

He said, "Time will help heal you but your actions are hurting a lot of people." He was crying.

I was hurting, and I did not care about anyone else's problems. When Daniel released my horse, I rode back toward the Stuart's house. Something compelled me to take the overgrown path to the woods. The sky was dark but no rain fell. My Oak Tree was

61

calling me. Other than the time I put my angry letter into the knot hole of a nearby oak tree, the last time I had been in those woods was with Father, the day before he left for Mississippi.

Once when my father finished saying prayers, we saw a squirrel watching us from that same knot hole. I knew where the big, beautiful oak was. When I got to Our Oak, somehow the tree did not look special. I even had trouble remembering why we had decided it was "Our Oak."

The circle of stones was still there. At first I thought some of the stones were missing, but they were just covered with leaves. I dismounted, stooped, and brushed the leaves from the stones. My horse put his head down and pushed me. I fell flat on the ground. Daniel, a short distance away, watched me. I sat up quickly so he would not come over to check on me. I was in the middle of the circle of stones, facing the oak tree that still did not look much different from the other trees. None of the trees had leaves—it was too early in the spring.

I remembered the magic circle Father and I had left near our cave last spring. Father had said, "Someone who needs direction for their life may find it in this circle." Sitting straight up with my legs flat on the ground and my hands in my lap, a vision came, a very clear vision. I saw a jar laying on its side with "MASON'S PATENT, NOV 30th 1858" printed in its pale blue glass, similar to the jars we had used for canning last summer after the hail storm.

Inside the jar was a chrysalis. I heard the chrysalis stir. In my vision, all five of my senses were active. Slowly I saw yellow and black wings emerge. The shell of that cocoon opened and a beautiful butterfly was born. The butterfly struggled and stretched its wings. I had never been that close to anything so beautiful. I said, "You are free, fly, fly."

The yellow and black wings were so big they touched the sides of the jar. Although the jar had no lid, the butterfly did not seem to know how to get out. How could I help? This was just a vision. I had not been able to control anything I had seen before. I had not saved Father or Slim or any of the other people I had seen and heard in my visions.

I heard my voice say, "Please, God, let me help." Then I saw my hands reach out, pick up the jar and guide the butterfly to safety. I put it on one of the rocks. It sat still, struggled some, took off on a short flight, then flew about ten feet. Soon it circled above my head and was gone.

I smiled, I laughed. I do not think I giggled, but maybe I did. My vision was gone. I was amazed, I still sat there. Then a single beam of sunlight came from behind me, lit up the oak tree and made it a thing of beauty. To me the sunbeam was a sign from God that even though my life had been full of darkness, my vision told me, brighter times were ahead of me. Only I, with God's help, could displace the gloom that I had allowed to control my life.

I scrambled up, ran from the magic circle straight to Daniel with my arms outstretched. He dropped his sketch pad and caught me in an embrace. Laughing, talking with my face pressed against his chest, I was so excited I could hardly breathe. Talk came so fast from me Daniel could not understand what I was saying.

He held me, sharing my joy.

Feeling tension draining from both our bodies, I told him about Father and building the circle near our cave then building the circle near the oak tree. I said, "We built a magic circle."

The magic was, if we ever needed direction for our lives, we should sit in it and ask for God's help. Then I told him about my horse pushing me into the circle and about my vision and the beautiful sunbeam.

Daniel said, "I saw your butterfly and your sunbeam."

"No, you could not have seen them, they were part of my vision," I said.

He stooped down and picked up the sketch pad he had dropped. He handed it to me without a word. No longer did I doubt he had seen my butterfly or my sunbeam. The drawing was of me in the magic circle with a large butterfly just over my head and a beam of bright sunlight lighting up a perfectly formed tree.

I was amazed. I had heard that sometimes life's greatest joy comes in a moment. Daniel had captured my moment.

The Mason jar was not in the sketch. We walked over to the circle to look for it. The jar was not there. The jar had disappeared along with my gloom. Of course the jar was never there. It was only in my vision. But the butterfly was there in Daniel's sketch.

Daniel and I rode back to the house. As soon as we entered the house, I started talking about my vision, about my Father, about our cave life, about any and every thing. I whirled, ran, laughed, caught D.T. and swung him around as Father used to do to me. The whole farm—except James—joined in my joy.

This attitude lasted three days. On the fourth of April, I woke up a little more subdued. I did not feel like a little girl anymore. I had a future and I must prepare for it. In the kitchen stove I burned the hate letter I had written to Missus Stuart. Daily, one a day, I burned all of those letters except the one I could not retrieve from the knot hole in the oak tree, burning them without reading them. I could not give up all my hate at once, I had to work through it. Complete freedom from my grief did not come immediately.

The weather was a big help. After a dark, gloomy, damp winter the sun came out. Yellow flowers showed up everywhere, yellow bellwort, yellow violet, buttercup, Solomon's seal. I am not sure the winter was really dark or if it was just the way I felt in my grief.

School did not seem quite the same as it had before my father died, but it was better than it had been during my bitter winter. Rosa and I did not regain the close relationship we had the summer and fall before. My self-respect returned. In class I was very careful with my appearance and I again became a "challenge."

I began a friendship with a new girl in our class, Jenny Vee, who could hardly keep up with even the worst student in class. At recess one day I saw her with an English book. She was bent over the book, crying. She looked up as I approached and sat beside her. I said, "Jenny Vee, what can I do to help?"

She said, "Teach me to read."

Taking her in my arms, I held her until she stopped crying. She was a small, pretty, but very sad person. As we talked, she told me she had five sisters and four brothers. Her father was a hired man on a small farm, and they had recently moved to the area. The pay for her father was mostly the right for them to live in an old run down house and food the farm owners gave them. Her father did make some money cutting timber for another man. She was worried about her mother and father.

She told me, "Mama and Papa are so thin and tired all the time." She also said, "Mama can read and we all get together every night. Mama reads the Bible to us and prays. Papa prays too.. He prays a real long time every night." She frowned. "I think if they prayed less and slept more they would be better off."

Before we went back to class, I said to Jenny Vee, "Tomorrow I will bring a book that is easier to read. We will find time together to study it."

There was no shortage of easy reading books at the Stuarts. Missus Stuart gave me about twenty books that Annie Margaret and D.T. were no longer interested in. I took five of them to school the next day. The teacher gave Jenny Vee and me permission to go into a small room off the hall and study together for two hours.

The teacher said to Jenny Vee, "I know it is hard for you to keep up with the class. I am sure Cleo can help you."

Jenny Vee was a fast learner. She did not catch up with the best of the class but before the school year was over, she was no longer the worst.

When Missus Stuart told the church what a hard life Jenny Vee's family was having, the congregation got involved and provided help. The family that owned the farm on which Jenny Vee's family lived had very little of their own. This was the first year they had a hired hand. The people of the church, nearby farms and some town people went to the farm. They brought food, clothes, books, toys, lamps, coal oil, seeds, and even coal. Some of these were given to Jenny Vee's family and some they gave to the family that owned the farm.

Most of those people had started their lives in that area with help from their neighbors. They knew two men would not be able to put in much of a crop so they came with horses, mules, plows, saws and other farm tools. They brought whatever they thought they could use to help the farmers get their spring crops started.

After a short time, Jenny Vee's family's garden began to bear. Jenny Vee told me, later, "Papa's prayers are just as long but they seem more hopeful."

Was it her father's prayers or Missus Stuart's words to the neighbors and town people that brought on the improvement in her father's attitude?

As spring came I spent more time around the barn with Ole Joe and riding the farm with Jed and Daniel. You might be surprised at how much work a ten-year-old farm girl can do.

One job all the men hated to do was clean the manure out of the chicken house. That became my job. Missus Bell liked chicken manure married with cow and horse manure spread on her garden soil. I kinda liked the closeness of working in the chicken house. There was a soft, feather, warm smell. The odor of the chicken dropping did not bother me. I would think of the beautiful vegetables and flowers they would help produce once we mixed them with compost.

In the garden, Missus Bell's pride and joy were her "bell" peppers. They were the biggest and best grown anywhere in the county. She planted her bell and hot pepper seeds in early spring and kept them in different windows in the house until the moon was right to plant them outside. Missus Bell had lots of help with her garden but she was the only one who decided when to plant. She knew the position of the moon even on cloudy nights. The spring of eighteen hundred and fifty-nine came early. The garden was plowed and the chicken manure compost had been mixed in the soil. The moon was right.

She handed James the hot pepper plants and said, "Listen carefully. This is very important. Plant these hot peppers in the row I dug near the barn." She added, "If the hot peppers are planted too close to my bell peppers, the peppers will cross-pollinate and my bell peppers will be hot."

James took the plants and said, "I understand, Missus Bell. I heard you say that a million times." He took off toward the garden.

Annie Margaret came up and said, "I want to help. What can I do?"

Missus Bell gave her the sweet bell pepper plants and told her about the row she had dug near the house. "These plants are special. I do not want you to plant them. Just drop each plant twelve inches apart and Cleo will come along and plant them."

When Annie Margaret got to the garden, James was waiting for her. He handed Annie Margaret the hot pepper plants and told her where Missus Bell wanted them planted. Annie Margaret was pleased to be given such an important job. She put them with the plants she already had. She dropped the plants very carefully twelve inches apart, measuring each one with a string on the row near the house. Then did the same thing on the row near the barn.

I came up to do my part of the job of planting the plants in the ground and watering them. I said to Annie Margaret, "Missus Bell will be so proud of you. Every plant is exactly twelve inches apart."

By the time it was discovered that the plants were mixed, they had blossomed. Missus Bell's bell peppers were almost as hot as her hot peppers. The pickled bell pepper and relish she was famous for could not be made. Everyone blamed James.

The day after planting the peppers, James, Annie Margaret and D.T. were seen by Ole Joe playing Ring-Around-the-Rosie behind the barn in the nude. Shoes were all they wore. Ole Joe went to the kitchen door, called out to Missus Bell and said, "Come quickly with me to the barn."

He did not tell her what he wanted her to see. The children laughed and giggled as they played the simple squat game.

Missus Bell took off her apron and wrapped it around Annie Margaret. Annie Margaret said, "Have you already washed our clothes?"

"Why? What has washing clothes got to do with you dancing with no clothes on?" Missus Bell asked.

The little girl said, "James said you wanted to wash our clothes and that we should take them off and go behind the barn and play."

All winter the people on the Stuart farm had been watching me in my grief. Now they had to start watching James in his insanity.

At first we thought James was trying to get attention. After all, he was a middle child. First born and last born children seem to demand less care but receive more. Last summer Rosa and I had spent a lot of time trying to get away from him. Sometimes we were mean to him, saying things like, "Leave us alone, James, we don't want you to come near us."

Ole Joe was put in charge of watching James when he was outside the house. During the daylight hours, I spent a lot of time at the barn so I watched James while Ole Joe milked the cows in the evening. A week after the children were found dancing in the nude, Ole Joe was milking and I was watching. Well not really watching as James had been just sitting still by the barn door for about an hour. My mind drifted to a poem I had read the night before about a dying cowboy.

A scream from James made me look up. He was running toward me with a look of real fear and hatred on his face. In his upraised right hand he held a hammer. I scrambled to my feet yelling and ran away. Ole Joe heard me and burst through the barn door trying to catch James. A root from a long dead oak tree tripped James and he fell flat on his face.

James' face was bloody and he was angry. He said, "Cleo was trying to dig out my eyes. I had to protect myself."

After that when Ole Joe could not give James his full attention, Jed or Daniel were there to help.

Once James, Missus Stuart, Ole Joe and I were inside the barn, James walked into the tack room. We knew there was no way out except through the open door he entered. We were talking about the mix-up in Missus Bell's pepper plants when we heard body slams. James was slamming his body against the wall of the tack room. He did this four times before Ole Joe could catch and hold him. James was only nine years old and small for his age but it took a while for Ole Joe to control him.

Missus Stuart said, "James, what were you thinking?"

"Ole Joe locked me in the tap room. He kept me there four days. Mother, he is a mean man."

Chapter 9

Doctor Johnson had been told about the situation sometime before and had examined James and had prescribed medication. This medication helped at times but made James sleep a lot. The doctor said, "I do not know of anything I can do except give him more of the same medicine. You should take him to see Doctor Harris. He will try to mesmerize James and see if he can find out what is causing him to act the way he does."

Mister Stuart asked the doctor, "Where is this Doctor Harris?"

"He has his practice in Indianapolis, so you can go and come back the same day by train." Doctor Johnson continued, "If you leave the day after tomorrow, I will be free to go with you." Looking straight into Mister Stuart's eyes, he said, "Dan, will you walk out to my horse with me?"

The two men left together. Doctor Johnson stopped half way to where his horse was tied, turned toward Mister Stuart and said, "Dan, I think you must prepare yourself for some very bad news." He paused, looked toward his horse, then turned back to Mister Stuart. He lowered his head and his voice. "It appears to me that James has cancer."

He hunkered down to the ground. So did Mister Stuart. The doctor continued. "The eyelid on his right side does not close completely. This indicates to me that there is a tumor pushing on his right eyeball. Doctor Harris is studying cancer and has had some success with mesmerizing patients for the examination he does through their eyes. If he cannot mesmerize them, he uses ether to put them to sleep."

"If you are right that James has cancer," Mister Stuart said, "What can this Doctor Harris do to treat him?"

Doctor Johnson pursed his lips and shook his head. "I really do not know, Dan. But if I am right, at least we will know."

The doctor advised that James not be medicated for the next two days so the medication would not interfere with the examination.

The following day was one of James's more normal days. He said, "Ole Joe and I can go horseback riding. I have not been riding in a long time."

Mister Stuart took him to the barn and behind his back shook his head to Ole Joe when James said, "Ole Joe, Father says I can go riding if you will go with me."

Ole Joe said, "My back is hurting real bad. It hurts me to stand, there is no way I can get on a horse today, but you hang around me for a while. We will clean and oil your saddle so it will be ready for you when my back gets better."

That seemed to satisfy James.

Mister Stuart saddled his horse to ride out to help two of the hired hands build a new bump gate for the upper pasture. James and Ole Joe watched as a red rooster strutted in front of the barn. A ray of sunlight broke through the overcast sky and shone on James. James made a sound almost like a rooster crowing then fell to the ground in a grand-mal epileptic seizure.

Mister Stuart and Ole Joe were by his side at once. They stayed out of his way and watched him thrash around. Mister Stuart did move a hoe and an old horseshoe that were on the ground near him. There was no part of James's body that was not jerking.

After the seizure James lay on his left side, still. He seemed not to breathe. He gasped, coughed and started breathing again. His father was crying when he picked him up and ran to the house with him.

Missus Stuart and Missus Bell met the two of them at the top of the kitchen steps.

James said, "Missus Bell, I am hungry. Was there any of that strawberry pie left?"

"You will not get any pie until you wash up. You are as dirty as a pig. How did you get so dirty?"

"I stumbled over an old hoe in the barn yard." He had no memory of his seizure.

The two women had watched his seizure from the back porch. His mother had started to go to him but Missus Bell said, "Dan and Ole Joe will take care of him. James probably will not remember what happened. Let them come to you."

After he ate a large slice of pie and drank a glass of milk, James and his mother went to the parlor. James started drawing pictures on his black board. He liked to draw ducks and drew a pretty good duck. He often said, "I can draw a better duck than that." Then he would erase the one he had just drawn and start another one. This day he erased his last duck and went and got in his mother's lap. He put his head against her cheek and giggled.

Missus Stuart said, "Tomorrow, you, Father, Doctor Johnson and I are going on a real long train trip, almost as far away as Virginia."

He kissed his mother's cheek, giggled again and said, "Father knows the man that runs the train, Mother. He is called an engineer. That man is going to let me ride to the next stop in the cab. I wish Father would not ride up front with me. I want to ride alone, but he said he had never ridden in a train cab and he was not going to miss his chance."

James looked so small when they left the next day for the train station. Nine years old and not as big as I was when I was seven. He had dressed himself in his best school clothes. Even though the day was warm, he had put on his winter jacket. In his hand he carried two bandanas, one red and one blue. Depending on which color the engineer wore, he was prepared to wear that color. The engineer and fireman wore bandanas around their necks to keep the coal dust from going down their shirts. None of us on the farm had seen James so happy in a long time.

Doctor Harris did not mesmerize James. He thought the examination was too painful. He put him to sleep.

James was very tired when they returned home. The next day, he began to talk about the "locomotive," he no longer called it a "train." He had learned a new word. We learned how coal was put into a locomotive, what kind of shovel was used by the fireman to put coal in the furnace of the locomotive, the sound and heat of the furnace, how the door of the furnace was opened by a foot peddle, that the engineer wore a blue bandana around his neck and the fireman wore a red one to keep coal dust from getting under their shirt collars.

School was still in session, and it was a relief not to have James going to school with us. His craziness had disturbed the whole school. Even the teachers were afraid of him. I continued helping Jenny Vee with her studies. Both Rosa and I tried to recapture our old friendship but the closeness was no longer there. Two days after school closed that spring, Rosa went to spend the summer with her aunt in Virginia. Lily went to Europe with two of her teachers and three of her classmates for the summer. Annie Margaret and I were the only girls left on the farm.

James required so much care and was so unpredictable that Annie Margaret and D.T. were taken to the Stonewall farm every day to play with the three Stonewall boys. D.T. loved it. Annie Margaret hated it until she met Nettie, the Stonewall's hired man's daughter. After that she even wanted to spend her nights there. Ole Joe would drive the two children over to the Stonewall's after breakfast and go get them before supper.

By this time James was spending most of his time in bed. Everyone in the household had a part in his care. Missus Stuart had a cot put in his room. She spent day and night with him. She seemed to age ten years in just three months. They hired a nurse but James would hardly let her near him.

Most of my time was spent either working in the garden, kitchen, or barn. James was convinced I was trying to dig out his right eye so I did not enter his room unless Missus Stuart sent for me. She called for me sometimes after James had been given a sedative. We sat together on the side of her cot and talked about what I had been doing. We watched James sleep but we did not talk about him. She also had private time with Daniel and Jed. She sat in the parlor every night for about a half hour before Bible reading and prayers with D.T. and Annie Margaret.

Late one afternoon Ole Joe and I sat on the edge of the bunk house porch. Ole Joe was carving a cow and I was whittling on a stick. I started to ask, "Mister Ole Joe—"

He broke in, "Cleo, please just call me Ole Joe. You are the only person in the world that calls me Mister."

I started, "My father—"

He pulled a strand of my hair and said, "Your father was a real gentleman, and I always called him Mister Lamb, but it makes me uncomfortable to be called Mister."

We were quiet for a while and then I started again. "Why are you called Ole Joe. It sounds almost like Old Joe?"

His knife became still, resting on the block of wood he had been carving. "Cleo, I will tell you about me."

I was always a good listener and I was ready to hear Ole Joe's life story.

"When I was about fifteen, I drifted up here from Kentucky. My brothers were all bigger and older than me. We did not get along. So one night I saddled up the worst, worn out horse we had and rode off. I came north to this part of Indiana. I was dirty, hungry, scared, almost ready to head back home when Mister Stuart and Mister Stonewall took pity on me and paid for some clothes, a bath, and a meal.

"They both offered me a job working cows on their farms. This was the daddy of Dan and Mister Stonewall was the daddy of three boys. Somehow it was Dan's father I rode home with. This bunk house was smaller then and there were already four hired hands here. I worked hard, learned a lot about cows and farms. Even learned how to read and write and some figuring.

74

Dan's mama would have two other hired hands and me come over and sit on her kitchen porch and teach us. I liked reading.

"Life was not all work and study. Sometimes after work some of us went to town. We call our trip to town 'girling'. You know that big house on the end of Main Street, all painted white? Well, that house is still there and it is still called the Girl House."

I broke in. "Yes, I know that house. That is where the pretty ladies live that get dressed up in fancy clothes and walk around town early every evening."

"Yes," said Ole Joe. "During the two years I stayed here, I did not go to the Girl house, although I did have a pretty little sweetheart in town named Beth. We were the same age, fifteen.

"I helped drive the cattle to the stock yards in Chicago the first year I was here. The cattle of the Stonewalls and the Stuarts were handled as one herd and we boys had a high old time riding together. Before the next year's drive I told Mister Stuart I wanted to try my hand at city living. The Stuarts had kept a true account of the monies I had earned and I had spent very little. The only real thing I had bought was a saddle. So I had a pretty good pocket full of money. The horse I was to ride in the drive was a good working one. Mister Stuart said the horse was part of my pay.

"Just before I saddled up for the drive Missus Stuart came out bringing a new red saddle blanket. As she handed it to me she said, 'This is for you. You will be welcomed if you ever want to come back to us.'

"No one had ever been as nice to me as the Stuarts. She hugged me and she did not see my tears.

"My time in Chicago was five years. Mister Stuart arranged for me to meet the owner of a large clothing store. He gave me a job. I was a clerk for six months, then was made department manager. Every year when it was time for the Stuarts and Stonewalls to bring their beef cattle to market in Chicago, I was there to greet them. I tried to like living in the city. I had a girlfriend. We went to concerts, plays, and dances but my mind kept coming back to this farm."

Ole Joe had a faraway look; I thought he was going to quit talking.

Then he continued, "It seemed despite the efforts made, city living was not to my liking. The fifth year when they came I was ready, packed and had quit my job and had said goodbye to my girlfriend and all the people I knew. I was even staying at the roadhouse the boys used when they were in Chicago.

"When my horse stopped at this bunk house, I knew I was home. My sweetheart of five years before had gotten married by this time, had two sons and was living in a town three hours ride away. I kinda forgot about her and started girling with the rest of the boys. We each had a favorite girl but if she was busy we would pick another one. They all seemed to know the same tricks."

I wanted to interrupt him and ask him what those tricks were but it was getting dark and I wanted to hear the reason he was called Ole Joe.

He must have read my mind for he said, "When I got back to the farm there was a young chap called Joe sleeping in the bunk that used to be mine. He was called Joe so I was called Old Joe. Dan started calling me Ole Joe and it stuck.

"After about a year I got tired of girling and went looking for a woman of my own. There were more men looking than there were women. I managed to find a few. One I even took to church two Sundays in a row. She, along with everybody in church, thought a wedding was in our future. Somehow I could not think of leaving this bunkhouse.

"Years passed.One day I heard that the husband of Beth, the girl I loved at fifteen, had gone to the gold fields of California the year before and taken their two sons with him. One Friday after I finished milking I rode the three hours to the town where she was living. A dance was going on. I loved to dance so I went into the building. Yes, I was looking for Beth and I found her. After that the last Friday of the month, I rode over to Beth's town and stayed with Beth until Sunday morning. She always went to church on Sunday and worked all week at a hat factory. I got back here mid-morning on Sunday. She never heard from her husband or sons.

"Beth is still there. I only see her twice a year now. Relationships change, people's needs change. She does not work in the hat factory now. The man she works for brings her already-made hats and she puts feathers, beads and stuff on them."

I sensed that was the end of Ole Joe's story. My mind went back to the many Friday nights Missus Bell had come to stay with me when Father would be away. Was he girling?

Missus Bell came out on the kitchen porch and called to me. "Cleo, you have already missed supper. You are not allowed to miss prayers. Come in the house now. You can talk to Ole Joe another time."

Chapter 10

*T*he family was gathered in the parlor when I rushed in. Missus Stuart's family used the parlor every day. Some family parlors were only used on special occasions. Mister Stuart waited for me to get my usual seat before he read the second chapter of Galatians. I do not believe he, himself, heard or knew what he was reading. None of us would think of much except the boy who lay dying in the bedroom down the hall. After the Bible reading, as was our custom, we held hands in a circle to say our prayers aloud. The oldest spoke first.

Missus Bell's prayer was beautiful. "God, please extract the hurtful thorns of habit from us and let us know Christ lives in us and please give us faith in the Son of God, who loves us and gave himself for us."

Mister Stuart's prayer was one we had heard him say many times before. It was based on a couple of verses from Hebrews, sixth chapter. "Sometimes seasons are dry and times are hard, but God you are in control of all things. You are our divine refuge. You are our only hope."

Missus Stuart's prayer was brief. "Thy will be done."

Jed, Daniel and my prayers were spoken very softly. I do not think even God was able to hear them.

Annie Margaret said, "Jesus, God please let James play Ring Around the Rosie with D.T. and me again." She spoke in a strong, clear voice.

Using the same tone of voice, D.T. said, "Jesus wept."

Then most of us wept. We were remembering lots of times in prayer we had been angry with James because he would disturb our prayer service by saying, "Jesus wept," sometimes over and over, very loud while he laughed and giggled, getting out of his chair, running around. Once he accidently turned his chair over and got tangled up in the rungs.

Missus Bell told me my supper was in the warming oven. My mind was on other things. I forgot to eat supper. I wondered was it God's plan for Ole Joe to live the life he led? If he had not gone to Chicago, would he have married Beth? Where were Beth's husband and children? Did Father go girling? If Father had not gone to Mississippi, would God have taken his life anyway? Why was James born? Why had God made James so mean and so sick? Was James being punished by God for some sin committed by Mister or Missus Stuart? In Ephesians, chapter four, we are told that we are of one body with different functions and elsewhere we are said to be a piece of the divine puzzle with a mission that no one else but us can fulfill. Did James fulfill his mission? "Yea though I walk through the valley of the shadow of death." Was God with James now? Psalm twenty-three said he was.

I was almost eleven years old. Since my vision of releasing the butterfly from the Mason jar, which I had interpreted to mean that even though my spirit had been injured or confined by the grief I felt after the death of my father, it was up to me, with the help of God, to transform my life into something free and beautiful like the butterfly. Was death the way God was helping James to fulfill his mission? What was my mission? Would God help me fulfill my mission? If I read the Bible from Genesis to The Revelation, would I get the answers for which I was looking?

Doctor Johnson came early the next day. He spent a long time in James' room with the nurse and Mister and Missus Stuart. After he left, Mister Stuart came out of James' room and told Missus Bell, "Please go get Ole Joe. I want him to go after Rosa. James has a very short time to live. Maybe she would like to see him before he dies. Ole Joe is to give her a choice. Come home now or later—it will be up to her."

Missus Bell said, "If I were twelve I would want to come. Death comes to all things even the mighty oak."

That was the first time I had ever heard Missus Bell speak of an oak tree. Then I remembered her father had come to America from Wales. Celtic blood runs deep.

Ole Joe left by train for Virginia to get Rosa. I knew she would come, she really loved James. She just hated the mean things he did. She had told me what a beautiful good baby and small child he had been. She had cared for him, as Annie Margaret cared for D.T., until he was about eight years old when he began to change. D.T. was just a baby when the first instance with James was noticed. Missus Bell was sitting with D.T. in her lap, D.T. was sucking his own fingers, when James pulled D.T.'s fingers out of his mouth and put his own fingers in. D.T.'s lips closed on James' fingers in a sucking motion.

James slapped the baby and said, "He is a snake and he bit me. Snake, snake, I am going to kill you."

After that incident Rosa said James would go for a week or two without doing something irrational. Then, when he had a mean spell, he would turn into a bully.

Rosa and Ole Joe did not get home before James died. Our Lutheran pastor came to the house as he often had during James' illness. This time he just stayed. He was not healthy himself. Just getting off his horse was tiring for him, but he wanted to be there to help in any way he could. We felt blessed by his presence and his prayers.

The nurse took care of the physical needs of James. He was on his left side to relieve as much pressure as possible to his right side—his right eye was almost out of its socket. He had been in a deep coma for three days and nights. Mister Stuart was there and in a daze. Missus Stuart looked so tired and the pastor was pale and trembling.

It was about two o'clock in the morning. Doctor Johnson came and took one look at the pastor and said, "Nathaniel, you have to get some rest." Then he turned to Missus Bell and said, "Missus Bell, will you please prepare a bed for this good man?"

Earlier Missus Stuart had asked me to come sit by her. She knew James was not going to be able to know I was there or to accuse me of trying to dig out his right eye. I knew I was a substitute for Rosa. At two thirty, Doctor Johnson left the room. He returned in a few minutes with Missus Bell, Jed and Daniel.

We all watched James. There were two coal oil lamps burning. One was close to the bed so the nurse could see the face of her patient. James coughed and mucus came from his mouth. The nurse was cleaning his mouth when he suddenly turned on his back. His left eye opened, his right eye lid could not cover his protruding eye. He started singing in a voice that everyone in the room heard. He sang, "Jesus loves me this I know, for the Bible tell me so." Then he sang in the same sing-song voice, "I love Missus Bell, I love Father, I love Mother."

It seemed that he was in our family prayer circle saying he loved each one of us. He went by age and included Lily, Rosa, Annie Margaret, D.T. He said, "I love Cleo," after he said, "I love Rosa." Then he said, "I love me," before he added Annie Margaret and D.T. While he was doing this with his left eye opened he seemed to be picking tiny things out of the air with his left thumb and forefinger.

None of us moved. He became quiet, not seeming to breathe. The nurse turned him back on his left side, we heard him breathing again. His respiration was noisy. We all knew this was what was called a "death rattle." He was very pale, almost blue.

Doctor Johnson reached under the covers, touched his feet and legs, then looked at the nurse and said, "It is over." James had breathed his last. He had done many mean things. Did that mean he was responsible for his sins or was his life part of God's plan?

Rosa and Ole Joe arrived on the morning train. James' body had been prepared and dressed for burial. He was laid on two wide planks between two straight chairs in the parlor. There were coins on both eyelids to keep them closed. If you looked closely, you could see where the nurse had clipped a tiny slit in both corners of his right eye in order to bring the eyelid down.

Missus Stuart thought it best to wait until his casket was brought from town before Rosa was allowed to see him. Rosa was very distraught. Doctor Johnson gave her a sedative and put her to bed. She and Ole Joe had spent the night on the train; she had talked and cried most of the night.

Missus Bell was in the kitchen cooking. That seemed to be her way of dealing with her sadness over the death of a child she had cared for all of his life. We really did not need any more food. Every family for miles around must have brought food. Baked ham, chicken, roast beef, pork, all kinds of vegetables, cakes, pies. Jenny Vee's family brought food they should have kept for themselves. Then company came. Missus Stuart's aunt and cousins arrived from Virginia. People came, town people, farm people, the Stonewalls. Everyone wanted to give their condolences to Mister and Missus Stuart. Mister and Missus Stuart sat or stood in the parlor two days and two evenings with James' coffin open and surrounded by flowers. The odor of the flowers was so strong you could even smell them in the kitchen.

At least there was more than enough food to feed the people. Ole Joe and the farm hands were busy caring for the horses of the visitors. Beds had to be found for the overnight guests. I slept on a pallet of quilts on the floor while two guests slept in my bed.

The night before James' funeral at Bible reading I read Second Corinthians, first chapter, fourth verse "that God comforts us in all our troubles, so that we could comfort others." But I could not see how all those people around could be a comfort to anyone. Would it not have been better if the members of the Stuart household had been left alone to bear their own grief?

James' funeral was held the next day in the Lutheran Church with burial in the church cemetery.

The sermon was based on First Thessalonians, chapter four, verses thirteen and fourteen, "We know that death brings sorrow and tears but our hope is in the risen Christ."

The Virginia cousins left the next day. Three days later Mister and Missus Stuart, Rosa, Annie Margaret and D.T. left on the train with Missus Stuart's aunt for Virginia. Mister Stuart returned home alone the same day. He went into his bedroom and stayed until Doctor Johnson came to check on him.

For as long as I had known the Stuarts, Doctor Johnson came every Wednesday for supper. After supper the two men would walk down to the bunkhouse and have a chat with Ole Joe and anyone else that might be there. Sometimes the hired men might be there, or maybe some of the boys from the Stonewall farm or the veterinarian might drop by. Later Mister Stuart and Doctor Johnson had a cigar, a drink of Kentucky whiskey and played chess in the library.

The night Mister Stuart came back from Virginia, the two men stayed in the library until after twelve o'clock. Later, I heart Doctor Johnson helping Mister Stuart to his room. Doctor Johnson's wife was still at her mother's and his son was at his boarding school.

Missus Stuart thought she had to choose between the well-being of her children and the care of her husband. It was not an easy choice to make. Mister Stuart told her that first duty, at that time in their lives, was to their children.

For three days we saw very little of Mister Stuart. When he did come out of his room, his walk was unsteady and his eyes were red and almost swollen shut. Doctor Johnson stopped by the afternoon of the third day. The two men went into Mister Stuart's office. In about a half hour, the doctor came out and asked Missus Bell to fix a pot of strong coffee.

For the first time in three days, Mister Stuart had supper with us—the first real meal he had eaten since he returned from Virginia. Ole Joe and Missus Bell had been running the farm since James had taken to his bed and Mister Stuart was not in condition to take over. Doctor Johnson spent the night and was there often after that. Instead of playing chess at night, they started playing cards. Pastor Nathaniel, Jed, Doctor Johnson and Mister

Stuart played until late in the night. Instead of Kentucky whiskey, they drank watered down glasses of Missus Bell's elderberry wine and ate lots of her walnut bread with fresh churned butter.

Slowly Mister Stuart came back to running the farm. He never regained all of his outgoing nature. He walked slower, his shoulders dropped a little. It took him two or three tries to rope a cow. Before James' death, he was proud of the fact he could get a cow in one try. His spirit was damaged—he thought his world was no longer under his control. Until Missus Stuart, Annie Margaret and D.T. returned in the fall from Virginia, the men played cards or chess three or four nights a week. Sometimes Ole Joe played in place of Jed, and sometimes Mister Stonewall sat in for Doctor Johnson. The Kentucky whiskey decanter was removed from his office and the farm life went almost back to normal.

Wednesday afternoons, neighborhood swims had been going on since the first of May. Jed and Daniel, some of the women from town, and some people from the Stonewall farm and neighboring farms went. Somehow I could not bring myself to go.

The fair came to town the first week in July, my birthday week. Last year, I had thought the whole world celebrated. There were only Missus Bell, Jed, Daniel and me staying in the farmhouse. Mister Stuart had gone to Virginia for the week. Lily was still in Europe. Missus Stuart, Rosa, Annie Margaret and D.T. were in Virginia. James was in his grave. If I was not sleeping, reading the Bible or helping Missus Bell with housework, I was with Jed, Daniel or Ole Joe doing outside work.

Doctor Johnson's son, Amos, came over often. He was in town for two weeks. I heard him say to Jed, "Mother could not come with me. Grandmother was having one of her spells. Grandmother seems to be able to do anything she wants to until my father is involved."

Jed just rolled his eyes and said nothing.

Amos continued, "I really think it is Mother who is sick and not Grandmother. Mother was raised in the city and never should have left it."

On my eleventh birthday, Jed came into the kitchen. I was reading the Bible to Missus Bell about Noah and the flood.

He handed me my hat and said, "Cleo, come on. We are going to be late."

I stood up. "Where are we going?"

"This is your birthday and you are going with three handsome young men to the fair."

My horse was already saddled. I imagined the midway, the weird people, the barkers with their crazy spiels, the food, the crowds. What I actually saw that year at the fair was the barns, farm, animals and equipment. They showed plows run by steam, a new kind of saw that hardly took any effort to cut up a huge log.

We never did get to the midway. While the boys were looking at the new breeds of cows, I wandered into the chicken display. I had never seen so many kinds of things with feathers. Some of them looked as though their feathers had been put on backwards.

Missus Bell entered only one thing in the fair—a black walnut cake. She won the blue ribbon. Ole Joe and I had cracked the walnuts. He had a rock with a small hole in it. He or I inserted the walnut, point side down, hit the top side with one sharp blow, and the nut almost always split in four pieces. That was fun. Missus Bell even complained the meat of the nuts was so large she had to break them up.

The Fourth of July gala was a big success. The band practiced their music often. The village had more dances that year than ever before. A young man, the son of one of the German men who came the year before, brought the German wine that was so popular with the grownups. His name was Alfred Bischoff. Everyone talked about him. To me he seemed to be a tall, shy man who could speak very little English but played an accordion better than anyone in the whole wide world.

The Stuarts' hired man, his wife, and the farm hands were the only ones from the Stuart farm to go to the gala. Most of the family members were still in Virginia and Lily was in Europe. The rest of us, Missus Bell, Jed, Daniel, Ole Joe and I did not feel comfortable celebrating so soon after James' death.

Doctor Johnson's wife and Mister Muller led the Grand March. Missus Johnson must have felt a Gala was worth leaving her "sick" mother since she had been asked to take the place Missus Stuart had the year before.

We were told that the most attractive young couple in the Grand March was Gretta Muller and Alfred Bischoff. They married later that year and he went to work in her father's store.

The family came back from Virginia a week before school started. Rosa was only home for seven days before she left for Missus Howard's Finishing School. One of Lily's teachers was offered a teaching job at an elite girls' school in Switzerland and Lily was accepted as a student there. The Stuarts offered to arrange for me to go with Rosa to Missus Howard's Finishing School. I was not ready for a change so I declined. I did not want to leave the farm.

Our lives settled down. Missus Stuart and Missus Stonewall spent a lot of time together visiting Doctor Johnson's patients, doing many things with the town women and church work. Annie Margaret and D. T, when they were not in school, needed very little care. Life became mostly routine. There are always things to do on a farm. I did some of everything and still found time to go to school, read my Bible, go to town, help Missus Bell, ride and follow Jed and Daniel around.

Our nightly Bible reading and family prayer service continued with me as a leader. Doctor Johnson came by the house three or four times a week. He and Mister Stuart were best friends.

One day the next summer I said to him, "Could I ride with you and drive your buggy, then you can get some rest."

He smiled. "Cleo, I'll do better than that. You come with me this afternoon, and pack a small bag."

I asked, "Where are we going?"

"We are going to help a mother deliver a baby."

I replied, "I can do that. I helped Mary Lee deliver a baby."

"Yes, I know you did. This time I want you to care for the patient's other two children while I help the mother."

He arranged with Missus Stuart for me to stay with the new mother's family for a week. That was the beginning. I became a doula giving emotional as well as physical support. Well, maybe not a real doula at first. Taking care of a household is not easy work. But with Missus Bell's day to day training, I had learned to delegate. The man in that family learned he could wash dishes, cook eggs and change diapers. The new mother was surprised at the things her six year old could do around the house such as make beds, sweep floors and bring in wood. Even the three year old had chores, bringing clean diapers and picking up toys.

That became my pattern. I loved it. I was boss and I got paid. Doctor Johnson was the one that collected my pay. I think sometimes the money came from his own pocket. My money manager was Mister Stuart. He had already told me Father left money with him and that Father's insurance money was always available for anything I wanted. What did I have to spend it on? Material for the clothes I made for myself, shoes, a gift once in a while. My needs were few.

My twelfth, thirteenth, fourteenth and fifteenth years were busy ones with school, church, my work with Doctor Johnson and the things I did around the Stuart house and farm. I was happy. I felt useful. Lily got married, Rosa went to school in Europe and Daniel took off to an art school in Philadelphia. That left Mister and Missus Stuart, Annie Margaret, D.T., Missus Bell, Jed, Ole Joe, the farm hands, the hired man and his wife and their two children and me on the farm.

One day in my fifteenth year, Doctor Johnson was called on an impending birth. I went along to help in any way I could. The patient's sister was going to help with the actual birth. I was outside the house cleaning the brass on the doctor's buggy when Doctor Johnson came to the door and called to me, "Cleo, I need help. I have a baby coming and my helper has fainted."

I caught the baby while Doctor Johnson took care of the sister that fainted. After that I carried my own black bag and was at the doctor's side on most every call he made. No one ever objected, or if they did, I was never told.

Sometimes one of our patients lived in the "Girl House." That was always interesting. There were lots of gold and velvet drapes, sofas, chairs, even the tables were painted gold. Our calls were made in the day time. Mostly I saw men at the bar drinking or playing cards at felt-covered tables. Some of these men I knew either from town or nearby farms. Doctor Johnson never stopped to visit with those men in the Girl House as he would have if he met them on the street. The girls we met would smile and say "hello" or "good morning" and looked like other girls I knew during the day. They did not look like the same girls I had seen on their evening stroll.

With Daniel gone, Jed and I spent a lot of time together on the farm, sometimes going to church dances or parties together. If Daniel had been there, the three of us would have been together.

After my sixteenth birthday, at the fair and annual Fourth of July gala, Jed said, "Cleo, Grandmother and I will be leaving for Arizona the second week in August."

I said, "That is a terrible time to go to Arizona. It is so hot there."

He said, "Forget the weather. What I want to know is will you go with us?"

This question was no surprise. I knew about the Bells's plans to move west. Missus Bell's niece Mary Lee and her husband Richard Poe had written many times about the big ranches and big herds of cattle there. Jed's dream had been to own more beef cattle than Mister Stuart. Mister Stuart had cut way down on the yearlings he bought and put more of his farm into corn and food crops.

Jed said, "When you get to be a little older, we could get married and start a family of our own."

I don't blush, but I blushed then. I said, "Give me two days. I want to talk to Missus Bell and Missus Stuart." I was tempted. Daniel was gone and now I was losing Jed. They both were a big part of my life. They were my best friends. Since my father's death, they had been my closest companions.

Missus Bell and Missus Stuart and I had a long talk that evening. They both were so kind. We even cried together. Each of us felt sorry for ourselves.

That farm had been Missus Bell's home for thirty-five years and she had known Missus Stuart for twenty of those years. It was the only home I ever had. The first nine years of my life, except for the first two years, I had never spent a year in one place. My father and I just moved on.

I did not wait two days. I told Jed that night, "I will always love you. I also love Daniel, but I am not ready for a commitment. My interest right now is to become a midwife."

The Stuarts had parties, dinners and gifts for the Bells before they left for the west. The Bells had saved enough money for a real good start on an established ranch that Richard had found for them.

I received my very first real kiss. Jed kissed me just before he left. A strange feeling came over me. My body was responding to something my head was not aware of.

Chapter 11

*F*or two or three years the girls at school had talked about a "witch" that you could go to if you got pregnant and she would take the baby away from you.

Doctor Johnson briefed me. "Missus Putman is not a witch. She grows herbs and is a healer. Some of the treatments I use, I learned from her."

I still thought I would see a witch with lank grey hair, stooped shoulders and moles. The lady that met us at her log cabin door was medium build, dressed in a nice, clean, starched and ironed blue dress. She was one of the neatest people I have ever seen. Her soft brown hair was in a braid coiled around her head. She looked to be about forty years old. Her house and garden were as neat as she was.

Doctor Johnson liked to surprise me. This time he really did. The mother to be was Starr, the "star" of the Girl House. Starr was walking around, her contractions had started during the night and Doctor Johnson had been alerted.

He said, "Cleo, come visit with Starr while Missus Putman and I go look at her herb garden."

Starr treated me like an honored guest. "Missus Stuart, would you like honey or sugar in your tea?"

Smiling, I corrected her as I had so many people over the years. "My name is Cleo Lamb. I am not a Stuart. I am a ward of the Stuarts."

She gave me the best chair in the house. I continued, "Please call me Cleo, I would like honey in my tea."

We discussed the weather, what Ole Joe had been up to, how much time I spent with Doctor Johnson. During our second cup of tea, she had a contraction. Not a bad one but she bent over in her chair and was rubbing her back. I had seen enough births to know where her pains were. So, I stood behind her and massaged her back. When the pain passed, I massaged her neck and shoulders.

"Cleo, that feels so good you can keep it up all day. '

I asked her, "Do you want a boy or a girl?"

She answered, "Neither. I do not even want to see this baby." She moved to the edge of her chair so I could get to her back easier. "Let me tell you about this baby. There are six men in our town that think this is their baby. They have been giving me extra money for eight months." She smiled. "I'm thirty-five years old and getting to old to work in the Girl House. Men and I have been girling since I was sixteen and I love my job. I put passion into every trick I turn."

I did not interrupt.

"I never turn any man away, and believe me, I've enjoyed every one of them. This all started as far back as I can remember. My father started off tickling me. From that he went to blowing bubbles with his mouth on my skin. By the time I was four, night time was happy time. He put a lock on my bedroom door when we were alone together. My mama was scared to death of my papa. I am sure she knew what was going on but she did not interfere. Papa made good money at the saw mill and people in town thought we were a good Christian family. I guess we were. I sure was happy. I have an older brother. When I was about seven and he was nine, I showed him what he could do to please me."

Another contraction started. I massaged her back but did not interrupt her story.

When she was comfortable again, she continued, "Having one man and a boy was enough for me until my brother got the idea of inviting sixteen boys to my sixteenth birthday party. The party was almost over when Papa found out what we were doing. He came in like a bull. The boys scattered and he told my brother and me never to darken his door again. The only place I knew to go was the old witch's house."

Missus Putman and Doctor Johnson came in the room while Starr was still talking. Starr said, "Doc, what have you and the old witch been doing?"

Doctor Johnson said, "We are waiting for you to have this baby."

Missus Putman went over to Starr, helped her up from her chair, gave her a hug and a long kiss on the lips and said, "Dear, let's walk around the room a while and see if we can't hurry this baby along."

While they walked, Doctor Johnson and I talked. "Starr says she does not want to even see this baby. What is going to happen to it?"

"There is a woman that lives over in the next county. She has been pretending for seven months to be pregnant. She made herself vomit for a while, put pillows under her dress of different sizes as though the baby was growing. She knitted blankets and made clothes. I think she even convinced herself she was going to have a baby. I know she convinced her husband. Missus Putman arranged all of this."

I was so surprised. I know my eyes were big and my mouth was open.

"Judging by Starr's condition, the baby should be here before very long. The woman that is going to take the baby has been sent for.

Missus Putman had everything well-planned. She and the doctor decided to use a birthing chair. After Starr's water broke, the birthing process went well, and a healthy boy was born. While I was bathing the baby, Missus Putman went outside and returned with a package containing baby clothes and two blankets.

She said, "Missus R. gave me these and is pleased it is a healthy boy. She heard his first cry."

While Doctor Johnson was massaging Starr's stomach and waiting for the delivery of the placenta, Missus Putman took the tiny wrapped bundle and I watched out the back window as she handed it to a lone woman waiting beside a black buggy.

The woman pulled the blanket from the baby's face, looked at him, kissed his forehead and smiled.

I heard more of Starr's story later.

"When I came to this cottage, I was battered. Papa had beat me up pretty good plus some of those sixteen boys had not been gentle."

Missus Putman said, "All Starr needed was love."

Starr interrupted. "All I needed was men. I decided I could have my fun and get paid for it. A week later I was a member of the Girls Club at the Girl House. That was nineteen years ago."

Missus Putman said, "That is all over now. In a few days, we are on our way to New Orleans."

Starr broke in. "We have enough money to keep us in style until I can find me a rich husband. We are working on my story but we are pretty sure I will be the widow of a Confederate hero. This sweet old witch, here, will be my maid," Starr said as she looked lovingly at Missus Putman.

We were comfortable after we cleaned up everything and the baby was gone. A mint tea was served while Missus Putman heated up a late supper. It was a simple meal of roast pork, mashed potatoes, gravy, cornbread, green beans, hot biscuits and jelly. More mint tea was passed. This time, Doctor Johnson poured a generous amount of Kentucky whisky into all the cups but mine.

I asked Starr, "How did you keep from having a baby for all those nineteen years you were at the Girl House?"

Starr was sitting up in bed with Missus Putman in a chair beside the bed. She reached over and took both of Missus Putman's hands in hers before she said, "This sweet old witch has a magic wand. I would spend at least one night a month in her nice warm bed and let her work her magic."

They kissed each other as though there was deep love between them. Then Starr said, "After my thirty-fifth birthday, I got careless. Two and a half months passed before I came home. Witchie would not use her magic wand. She gave me all kinds of reasons including it was dangerous to me, it was God's will, it would reflect on her soul's journey. Anyway we started planning what we would do with the baby once it got here."

Missus Putman said, "Missus R. has been a patient of mine for two years. She and her husband wanted an heir. Everything they owned when they died would go to his younger brother, who they both hated. That is what she told me. But the truth is she wanted a baby to love, she has always wanted to be a mother."

Somehow I felt everyone in the room was pleased about the outcome of this birth. The baby was healthy. The birth mother was well and relieved that the baby was going to be loved and cared for. Missus Putman's plan had worked.

Doctor Johnson added another dollop of whisky to their fresh cups of mint tea.

I said, "How is this Missus R. going to present her new born son? When her husband comes in from milking, will she lift up her skirt and hand him a freshly bathed and dressed boy and say Here is your heir?"

"No," said Doctor Johnson. "She will come in from outside and say, 'this is what a stork dropped into my arms.'"

Missus Putman quoted, "She found him in the garden under a cabbage leaf."

I thought Starr's idea was the most beautiful. "While she was walking under the stars, a beautiful witch dressed in blue handed the baby boy to her and told her, 'This boy will be a joy to you all your life and his life will be a blessing to the world.' When the witch turns away, Missus R. will swear there were wings extending from her shoulders."

Missus Putman looked down at her blue dress while her hands smoothed the wrinkles from her lap.

With that Doctor Johnson said, "We have all had a long day. I have never had an evening I enjoyed more."

Missus Putman had arranged our sleeping space. I was to sleep on a cot in the kitchen. As I looked around, the place looked so peaceful. My thoughts went to, maybe, when Starr and Missus Putman went to New Orleans, I could move to this cabin, tend to that perfect garden and live happily ever after.

"What is going to happen to your home and garden when you leave?"

She patted me on my arm and said, "All witches do not live alone."

To me that statement solved two mysteries. One, how did Missus R. know when to come for the baby. Two, who was going to live in the house after the two women left for New Orleans.

In the morning, dew had left diamonds on all the spider webs all around the cabin. I could almost believe Starr's story that, indeed, an angel had brought the baby.

Back home, my next three days were busy ones. The hired man's wife came over every day to help with the cooking and housework. The house, to me, did not seem as clean or as cozy as Missus Putman's house. I talked Missus Stuart into letting me organize a full general cleaning. Even Ole Joe got involved, helping put the rugs on the line and beating them. Everybody worked. Annie Margaret and D.T. were good workers. The house was gleaming when we finished.

I put my collection of wood, metal and china butterflies in a drawer and started collecting stars. I could only find one star in the house and two spurs with stars on them in the barn. I rode into town and bought three more. I had started hooking a small rug with a butterfly motif. That butterfly got changed into a star. Starr and her stories were on my mind day and night. What did it feel like to make love? I remembered the feeling I got when Jed kissed me goodbye. Was that love?

Then I remembered Starr had not talked about love, but she had talked about how happy it made her feel to have intimate relations with a man. I was not sure she did not also have intimate relations with Missus Putman.

Curiosity is what drove me a week later to select the newest farm hand on the farm to go riding with me. Earlier that day I heard one of the other boys ask him, "Nathaniel, have you ever been girling?"

His reply was, "Sure, lots of times, that Starr is some woman."

That did it, his fate was sealed. He was not much older than me and not near as handsome as Jed, Daniel or Amos. But he was there when I was ready.

I planned well. Rosa and I had a hideout down near the river. James had never been able to find us when we were there. Over the years I had spent a lot of quiet reading time in that secret place. I preened and smiled at Nathaniel for about fifteen minutes then said, "Nathaniel, would you like to ride down to the river with me? I have no one to ride with and I am afraid to go that far alone." It was a good thing none of the other hired hands heard me because since Jed left I mostly rode alone.

Nathaniel and I went to the barn and saddled up our horses. My horse and I led the way to the river. As we dismounted I smiled what I thought was a fetching smile and said, "Nathaniel, I know a place no one else knows about. Would you like to see it?"

Most everybody loves secrets and by that time he would have followed me into the river if that was where I wanted to go.

After we entered my secret area and sat down, I laid back as though I was studying the vines overhead. Nathaniel was pretty nervous, not saying much. He saw me lying back so he did also.

I reached over and took his left hand in mine and asked him, "Do you really know Starr?" at the same time I rolled to my side, put my left arm across his body and kissed him. I had very little practice in kissing and somehow it seemed to me he knew less about it than I did. I had been kissed once by Jed.

Well, the truth is I seduced him. I wanted to know what "laying with a man" felt like. Over the years I had heard many stories from girls and women. Starr's story was the last one I had heard and she seemed to want every man on earth.

I was deflowered, but just barely. He rolled off me at once and said, "You are evil. You caused me to commit the worst sin in the world. You are evil, evil. You are in league with the devil."

I had to admit whatever we had done was my fault and if that was what "laying with a man" was it sure wasn't pleasure so it must have been sin.

He rode off as though he thought I would make him sin again.

He must have forgiven me for being in league with devil. Two days later he asked me, after he made sure we were alone, "I think we ought to try again."

My curiosity was still strong so I said, "Meet me down at the river in half an hour."

I got there first and loosened all my clothes. Nathaniel came in the secret place very nervous. I did what I could to help him. He seemed ready but he lasted less than a minute. I found no joy in that. He surprised me when he took out his Bible and started reading to me about the bad person I was.

He said, "Cleo, it is very important to me for us to meet Sunday night after the tent meeting."

I thought I had given this intimate relations thing a good try and was hoping this would be the last time we would be together.

Nathaniel and some of the other hired hands had been going to a religious tent revival every night for two weeks. So I should have been prepared for what happened. We met at the same place the next Sunday night. After he entered, he dropped to his knees and started praying for my sinful soul. He called all women bad. He said even his mother was stained with the sins of Eve. To be honest, he preached a pretty good soul-stirring sermon. He talked on and on. Sometimes his Bible quotation did not relate to anything he was talking about.

Truth be told, I went to sleep while he was still preaching. What woke me was him singing, "Bringing in the Sheaves." Then he sat down by me and started telling me again how evil I was and it was his job to save my soul. That was his mission, to save my soul that night. He was trying to pull me from Satan and keep me from the fires of hell. He repeated the same thing over and over. "Must save a soul from the pits of hell."

When he stopped to rest his voice, I asked, "Nathaniel, how long have you been in this area?"

"A month. I came here to visit a cousin and look for a job. This is my third week working for Mister Stuart, but I have found so much evil in this place I am not sure I will stay much longer."

Starr had not been girling at the Girl House for over six months. Nathaniel had heard about her but had never been near either Starr or the Girl House. He knew less about intimate relations than I did.

The next morning Ole Joe told us that Nathaniel had left the farm. He saddled up the horse Mister Stuart had assigned to him, packed a saddle bag and went to the revival tent grounds. He helped them break camp and left with them the next morning. He stole the horse and gear but Mister Stuart knew horse thieves would be hung if tried. So he did not even report the thief.

I spent the morning finishing the star rug I had started, then took the spurs back to the barn and gave the three stars I bought to the hired hand's wife. I took my butterfly collection out of the drawer and put the one star I had left in the drawer. Somehow I still had a feeling there was more to "laying with a man" than I had experienced with Nathaniel.

I have heard that a doctor can look into a girl's eyes and tell if she is a virgin. The next day I felt that Doctor Johnson knew what I had done. I handed him my hooked rug with a star in the center. I said, "I want you to have this."

He smiled with a twinkle in his eyes as he took the rug and answered me saying, "Some experiences are to be treasured, others forgotten."

I did not forget my experience with Nathaniel, but I did not repeat it.

Chapter 12

*T*he war between the North and the South had a great effect on our lives. Indiana as a state was not much interested in the conflict. There were few slaves in the state and none in our area. Article XIII of our Constitution stated that no Negroes or mulattos would be allowed to come into or settle in Indiana without a bond being paid for their care. Some of the people in our area had moved from Kentucky and Virginia and their sympathies were for the South. Most of the young hired hands fought for the Northern army. Two of Mister Stonewall's men went back to Kentucky and joined General John Hunt Morgan's unit, a unit that later made a destructive raid into Indiana.

We in Arcidia were not raided by the Confederates. Three of our farm hands and our hired man went into the Union army. Daniel Stuart was in Philadelphia in art school. He was drafted and put to work making maps for the Union forces. He stayed in Philadelphia all during the war and was never involved in conflict.

When our boys left, Mister Stuart had just been south and bought his year's supply of calves to raise for beef cattle. We were short handed on the farm, so everyone remaining had to work extra hard. Ole Joe was still there and three older men who had worked in past times. Even Missus Stuart and the hired hand's wife and two children helped on the farm.

For four years the Union army bought most of the beef cattle raised on the Stuart farm. During the roundup, solders came and rounded up the cows and drove them to the train in Arcidia.

They sent twenty soldiers to do the job our four farm hands had done. Some of these soldiers did not even know how to ride a horse. Only one of them knew how to rope a cow.

We farm people enjoyed watching the action. I liked one of the young men. If I had not had my experience with Nathaniel, I might have accepted his invitation to walk by the river. I hope he survived the war and got back to his beloved Lake Pleasant, Pennsylvania.

Our three hired hands survived the war. The two Stonewall boys were not so lucky. One of them had a flesh wound in his thigh—a mini ball went all the way through his upper leg leaving a hole. He was recovering in a Rebel field hospital when he developed gangrene.

Once when his friend was visiting, he said, "We have changed a lot since we left the Stonewall farm and it seems I will never return."

His friend said, "We will take the low road together back to that old cow pasture. Don't worry, the doc is going to get you back on your feet."

That afternoon the friend was asked to hold the patient while the doctor rammed a red hot bayonet through the man's wound. After the patient fainted, the doctor turned the patient over and went through the flesh in the opposite direction with another red hot bayonet. He survived, the gangrene they feared was halted.

After the war he came back to the Stonewall farm, got married and raised four children. He became one of the Stonewall's main hired hands. That is, he was allowed to live with his family in one of the houses on the farm.

His friend was not so lucky. Three weeks after he helped with his friend's operation, he was killed. They say he was found, dead, lying across a fallen Confederate flag.

That summer a student at a university in New York from Greece came to spend the summer months with his uncle in Arcidia. He looked like Adonis and acted like Narcissus. He was exactly what I wanted for the summer. We made a deal, I would be his girl. He was sure all the women in town were after him and some of them were. Heads would turn when he walked into church. He loved the attention. The deal was that when we were together we would only speak Greek. Since my father died, I had only been able to speak in Greek to his uncle who ran a restaurant and he was always busy.

We even got so good together, at parties we would sing Greek duet songs and dances. Missus Stuart had a Greek style dress made for me. We led the Grand March at the Fourth of July gala. I have made that summer sound like a boy-girl summer but it really was not. I was using him to study Greek and he was using me to keep other girls and women away. He kissed me goodbye with two tiny kisses on each cheek. Neither one of us was sorry the summer was over.

Doctor Johnson was called to military service. He spent a year and a half as a battlefield doctor. His son Amos was a medical student when the war started and joined the medical corps. Amos went back to medical school after the war.

The war years were busy for me. There was no local doctor. People had seen me so often helping the doctor they came to me for help. I had access to his office and his books. I could not fill his shoes but I tried using pills I knew how to make and herbs I knew how to use. The local veterinarian was there to help me, to give advice and comfort. The midwife from the next county was sometimes available. Years before I had learned to delegate chores, so mostly I taught people to help themselves.

After the war years Mister Stuart started converting his farm to truck farming corn, potatoes, tomatoes, cucumbers, and peppers. Most of the rest of his farm was planted into wheat. He kept enough beef cattle for local sales and home use.

Church was a large part of my life. I was still the reader for the family prayer service at night. If I was not there, D.T. did the reading. Neither Mister nor Missus Stuart were as prayerful as they had been before James died. The phrases,"Thy will be done" and "Jesus wept" were not used in our prayers.

Through the years Missus Stuart's Uncle Frank visited us often. He still lived in Mississippi and had been successful in his business adventures. His visits always reminded me that he was the last family member to see my father. By that time I considered the Stuarts my family. I no longer corrected people when they called me Missus Stuart. They were the only family, except my father, I had ever known.

We received word just after my eighteenth birthday, July second, eighteen hundred and sixty-six, that Uncle Frank was very ill and had returned to Virginia to die. He never married. His estate was left to be divided equally between Missus Stuart's children, Lily, Daniel, Rosa, Annie Margaret, D.T., his two great nieces that lived in Virginia, and me.

Uncle Frank's funeral was very simple, just a graveside ceremony. He planned that no one was to be present except his family. He stated I was an honored member of his family, therefore should be there.

About three weeks later Mister Stuart asked me to come to his office. There were two lawyers, a money manager, Mister and Missus Stuart, and Doctor Johnson. I had been told that the meeting had to do with how I wanted my money to be managed. I had asked if we could include my friend, Doctor Johnson.

Since my father's death, I had signed any paper having to do with money with these same people present. The list and number of papers were much larger this time. Both lawyers and the money manager talked a long time about the amount of my inheritance from Uncle Frank and the investment I already owned. I signed every paper. Money had never been important to me and I trusted Mister Stuart's judgment. He never failed me. My stock in railroads, shipyards and coal made me a very rich woman.

Doctor Johnson returned to Arcidia from his war service a changed man. No person ever goes through trauma, either seen or experienced, without change.

After reviewing the charts and records I kept while he was away, he said, "Cleo, I am so pleased with the work you have done. At age eighteen, I could not have accomplished half as much as you have this past year and one half."

That compliment made me blush and stammer. Deep down in my heart I knew I deserved it. Besides doing my best, I had also studied his medical books.

In his office one day he said, "You are smart enough and have money enough I want you to consider going to medical school."

My answer was, "That would mean being away from home too long. I just want to be a midwife."

Two weeks later he said, "Sit down and don't argue. You are going to do this. There is a class starting next week in Chicago for advanced midwife study. It only lasts three months. I have arranged for you to enter this class and for you to live with my friend Doctor Harter and his wife Judy."

Chapter 13

I did not argue. I went home and packed only one suitcase knowing everything I needed could be bought in that big windy city. Ole Joe was so excited about me going. I believe he was almost ready to go with me.

Tears came often that week. I visited the magic circle under my oak tree but I did not enter it. Since I had helped the butterfly escape from the Mason jar, I had known my destiny was up to me and God.

Doctor and Missus Harter's house was large. There was too much space for the two people who lived there. My area was three rooms with a separate entrance. They had a housekeeper-cook, a maid and a gardener. They spent very little time at home. Doctor Harter was busy with his practice. Missus Harter helped him in his office plus was involved with a group that provided for the homeless people in Chicago. They welcomed me with open hearts.

Supper the first night was elegant, the table and service beautiful and very friendly conversation. The next night was the same service, except I ate alone, the same the third night. After that I asked Missus Harter if I could just go to the kitchen and prepare my own meals anytime I wanted. That became my living arrangement. I cooked for myself and made my own bed.

The class I attended had twenty women. All were experienced midwives. Everyone, except me, was over twenty-five years old. At first they treated me as though I was their mascot. I enjoyed being the baby of such a smart group of women.

The first teacher was a middle-aged male doctor. His first words were, "The sex act ..." then he paused, looked around the room watching our reactions.Then he continued, "The sex act is a coupling between a woman and a man. From now on in this class this act will be called sex. Sex is hereditary. If your mother and father had never had sex, there is a good chance you, too, will never have sex."

We laughed, relaxed and listened to the rest of his lecture. Up until that time, I had never heard of intimate relations being called "sex." To me sex was male or female. Female sex was girl, woman, hen, mare, cow. Male sex was boy, man, rooster, stallion, bull. Male or female was how all creatures were created by God. Sex was almost the same act that we called girling, only in Arcidia, girling could mean just visiting or walking out with a girl or woman. You could go play cards or drink at the bar in the Girl House and that too would be called girling. Mostly when the boys or men went to the Girl House, they went upstairs with a girl and paid her to have intimate relations.

There would be no midwives if there was no sex.

Before each class I went over the lesson. Most everything was taught from the books I already knew. I did learn a lot about how to teach. This teaching was very different from the Sunday school teaching I did in Saint Matthew Lutheran Church in Arcidia.

Two of our teachers could have gotten a job in New York City as entertainers. We learned from them and we also laughed with them. I had never attended classes with women before. I was a farm girl and thought I would be the dumb one among some very sophisticated ladies. The first day I wore my best clothes. I should have asked Missus Harter how to dress. All the other women wore morning clothes and brought large white aprons in their handbags. I was teased and asked if I was going to preach. The second day I dressed like the rest. I stayed up the night before until two o 'clock making an apron.

After two weeks of classroom work, we were each given a partner and told that Monday morning we would be doing field work. Field work to me had always been planting tomatoes or peppers. This field work was quite different. Half of us went to the hospital and others to private homes. My partner was Rebecca, a thirty-five year old married mother of two whose home was in an Italian section of Chicago. We had instant rapport and one day went with a doctor to a private home.

The mother-to-be was in labor when we arrived. Rebecca and I were only to observe. An elderly midwife and the doctor with us were to show us some of the things we had discussed in class.

The sister of the patient greeted us and invited us in. An older woman standing behind her lowered her head and murmured, "Good morning" in Greek.

For me, happiness lit up the room. I answered in her native language. She smiled, pushed the younger woman aside, opened her arms wide and gathered me to her bosom. She kissed me twice on both cheeks. We held each other in a close embrace. Somehow I felt I was embracing one of the long ago sisters that had cared for my father when he was growing up. It gave me such a warm feeling. Iona, the sister of the new mother, became my best Chicago friend. A single moment in life can last a lifetime. A smile or a hug can warm a whole winter.

For the rest of my three months in Chicago, Iona and I spent a lot of our free time together. She worked in her family's restaurant plus had a young man she was walking out with. In addition to my midwife classes, I took night classes in Latin, art and music appreciation. On Sundays, I went with Iona and her family to the Catholic Church. My father had told me that as an infant I was baptized, and before I was ten we sometimes went to a Catholic church. Almost always we attended a Christian church of some kind on Sunday. If that was not possible, we had our own service near an oak tree. After I released the butterfly from the Mason jar, I joined the Lutheran Church as that was the church the Stuart family attended.

Iona's mother gave me a beautiful black lace head covering to wear when I went to church. Although I attended regularly, I did not take communion or go to confession. The only thing I thought I should confess was my deflowering, and it was such a disappointment I decided it would always be my secret.

My three months in the big windy city went fast and included both work and play. Iona and I went to plays, concerts, parks, and sometimes ate in restaurants bigger than any building in Arcidia.

One down side was the days I spent with Missus Harter working with the homeless people. So many children had no one to care for them. One nine-year-old girl's hair was so snarled and dirty, it took me an hour to wash and brush it out. We fed her, bathed her, gave her clean clothes, then all she wanted to do was go to sleep. As I watched her sleep, I thought back to when I was her age. Then I had my beautiful father to care for me. Had we been in Chicago when he died I, too, might have been a street child. I could not leave her. Crying, I said to Missus Harter, "May I take this child with me to your house until we can find a better place for her?"

Missus Harter replied, "Leaving these people with so little hope is the hardest part of what I do. It seems the more we do the more there is to do." Looking over to the sleeping child she said, "You are in school every day. My job takes me away from home. The housekeeper says if I bring any more strays home, she will quit working for us."

I stood, turned my back to Missus Harter so she could not see my tears.

She patted my shoulder, turned me around and embraced me. "I attended an afternoon tea two weeks ago in our neighborhood in honor of a new arrival. This woman moved in with her elder sister. As I was talking with her I remember she said, 'Truly, I'm glad to be here but one thing I miss is my eight-year-old great-grandchild.'"

As I looked toward the sleeping child I knew Missus Harter would arrange for her to become part of the two sisters' household.

We took her home with us and she slept on a cot in my bedroom that night. Missus Harter went to visit the two sisters. The next morning the little girl moved into her new home. Years later she became Social Services Director for the City of Chicago and was responsible for the development of many homes for the elderly.

The midwife school taught me how to mesmerize, or hypnotize. They also taught me that a good pre-natal attitude by the mother to be was a great benefit. Happy mothers make happy babies.

⋄⇒⇐⋄

Willow, we should take a break from just telling my story. One question I know you have is, "Does Cleo still have visions?" Yes, I did during my time on earth. I did not outgrow them. I saw things that happened before my time, usually tragic things, shipwrecks, the black plague, earthquakes, sometimes the death of a single child, once an old man traveling alone in a desert. Some things I saw seemed to be happening at the same time I was seeing them, fires, storms, a volcano causing a large island to sink and creating four small islands. I saw a battle during the Civil War that many men were killed on both sides. It was not a victory for either the North or the South.

I did not see my own future. I did not see my marriage, the birth or death of my child, or my beautiful granddaughter. If I could have seen my future would I have changed things? I do not believe that it was in my power to change things. I believe a power greater than ours has our destiny in his hands. Sometimes my vision showed me the future. I saw the development of the railways as well as their decline. I saw air and space travel as you know them today. During your lifetime, Willow, you will be responsible for a scientific discovery that will make people remember your name for a thousand years and bless you for it. You will also witness a time when all the religions of the world will change.

⋄⇒⇐⋄

Iona's family had a large party for me before I left Chicago. Doctor and Missus Harter surprised me by knowing most all the Greek dances. Iona and her young man announced their betrothal at this party. Wine, food, music, dance—this party lasted for two days.

While I was in Chicago, many people from Arcidia and the farm wrote me about a new man in town. His name was John Tugman. He was living in an old army tent about a mile out of town. Everyone in town called him "John the Baptist." A man in our area that owned a farm deeded him ten acres of land to build a church. He was a Baptist preacher and had been told by his congregation in Kentucky to leave because he would not pray for the Confederates to win the War Between the States. His prayer to God was, "Thy will be done." The farmer that gave him the land had been a member of that church before he moved to Indiana.

John Tugman was a large man with a great message of salvation. Arcidia was growing; many Southern people were moving north and west to find land or work. The Lutherans and Methodists welcomed John the Baptist to Arcidia. His message of Christ would be given to people they could not reach.

Arriving in Arcidia I could see the new church from the train. It was painted white with a tall steeple. Daniel met me and as we drove past the church, I saw the sign, "Riverside Baptist Church. Reverend John Tugman, Pastor." I was impressed. Daniel said, "Everybody around has been helping that man build his church. He has the most persuasive manner."

I asked, "Even the Lutherans?"

"Oh, yes. Mother organized the ladies and as usual the women told the men what to do."

I laughed.

Daniel had been home from Philadelphia for four days. He looked particularly handsome as he had dressed up to meet my train.

I teased him and said, "You look as though you were expecting a very important person to get off the train."

He said, "The very most important person in my life did get off the train."

I could not believe my ears. My spine straightened, my neck got longer, my eyes got bigger, my lips parted. I looked into his beautiful blue eyes and saw a man when I had expected to see a boy. We talked very little the rest of the way home.

That night before prayers, I talked a mile a minute. Ole Joe came over from the bunk house to welcome me home. There were only Mister and Missus Stuart, Ole Joe, Daniel, D.T. and me for Bible study and prayers. Annie Margaret was at school in Richmond. Doctor Johnson came after prayers. All of us sat in the living room and talked until almost midnight.

Doctor Johnson said, "Cleo, you are near ready for your life's work. The war is over, the North and South are getting back together and so are the men and women. There will be more babies born in the next two years than have been born in the last ten years."

I hugged Doctor Johnson and said, "I am ready."

At breakfast the next day, Daniel said, "The family and I have talked it over. We have decided that we will take the two upstairs rooms in the new section of the house and make them into a studio for me." He added, "You want to deliver babies and I want to paint pictures. We can both do our lifes' work from this house."

I knew I never wanted to leave the Stuart family. His statement gave me a sense of contentment. I would be surrounded by people that loved and respected me and I was trained to do a job that I had dreamed of since my father told me about my mother and my newborn brother who had died when I was two.

D.T. , Missus Stuart, Daniel and I went to look at the two upstairs rooms. They were dark; stuff had been stored in them for years. Daniel pointed out where the new windows and skylight would be, talked about painting the walls and ceiling. He said, "After I paint the backdrop, Mother, I want you to sit for me dressed in the Stuart colors." Smiling, he turned to me and said, "Then I want to paint you holding a baby."

His voice was so tender it seemed to infer that the baby I would be holding would be his baby, not one I had helped another mother deliver.

Sunday came. Church was the same. Since I was nine I had attended that Lutheran church. The only difference this time was that Daniel sat beside me. First I had sat with my father. After he left for Mississippi, I sat between Rosa and Annie Margaret. When Rosa left, it was between D.T. and Annie Margaret. Daniel usually sat with the hired hands. During the first song, Daniel took my right hand in his and held it. He held my hand all during the service. It felt right and comforting.

The sermon was on the return of the prodigal son. My mind drifted to one of my favorite fantasy day dreams. In this dream, my father returned from Mississippi with a wife and three children, the oldest is a boy. I know I was trying to reincarnate the brother that was stillborn when I was two. The two younger children, in my day dream, were girls both about six or seven. One had the dark beauty of Rosa, her brown eyes bright and her body full of giggles. The other was like me. Our world was whirling, twirling, spinning, giggles and laughter. Moments and moments of pure happiness. I was so deep in my day dream Daniel had to pull me to my feet for the last hymn. I left church in a daze.

I remember some of my friends wanted to talk about my time in Chicago. They wanted to touch my new clothes, my hat and talk about me holding hands with Daniel. You may think people in a Christian church are only there to worship Christ, but fellowship is also a large part of what happened in church.

Chapter 14

*M*onday morning Missus Stuart, Daniel and I went to the kitchen porch together to see the new farm hand ride up on his horse. He was dismounting when we first saw him, his right hand was on the pommel, as his saddle had no horn. He shifted his weight slightly forward putting most of his weight on the left stirrup, swung his right leg over the saddle and stepped to the ground with his right leg. His left foot was hardly in the stirrup, just his toe, so it was easy for him to step to the ground. I had watched hired hands mount and dismount horses all my life. Somehow the action of this farm hand was in slow motion as though it was a moment I would remember forever—and it was.

He patted his horse's neck with his left hand, moved up to his horse's head and pulled his muzzle into his chest. I caught my breath. I heard Missus Stuart gasp. I fell in love with that farm hand's back. Every motion and gesture he made were the same ones I remembered my father making. From the kitchen porch, the view we had of him was as though we went back in time nine years. The muscles in his back and buttocks pulled his shirt and pants tight as he dismounted. The only difference in his dismount and Father's was that Father's saddle had a horn and his did not. His caress of his horse was the same as I had watched my father do.

Mister Stuart and Ole Joe came from the barn to greet the new farm hand. The man did not even see us on the porch. He led his horse toward Mister Stuart and Ole Joe. His back was still toward us. Without fully realizing what I was doing, I went down the porch steps and was ten steps into the yard before I came to my senses and stopped. I stood still for five minutes and just looked at the barn. When I turned around, Missus Stuart and Daniel were watching me.

At supper that night, I was quiet and asked no questions but Mister Stuart told us the new man's name was Walter Andrews, that he was a Confederate veteran from Kentucky. Before the war he had been a member of John Tugman's church. Walter was one of about twenty members that followed John to Indiana. He was a good carpenter and farmer who needed a job. The new River-side Baptist Church was almost finished and Mister Stuart want-ed to build another hired man's house. So it was going to work out well for both of them.

Crop farming took more workers than raising beef cattle and the Stuart farm had become a crop farm since more beef cattle were raised in the western states.

Tuesday, Wednesday, Thursday, I did not see Walter, although Tuesday I hung around the bunk house with Ole Joe most of the morning. Daniel came over to be with us. We had dinner with Ole Joe and three of the farm hands. Ole Joe said, "The other three farm boys will not be here to eat. They have gone to town with Mister Stuart to pick up material for the farm house they are building."

Daniel and Ole Joe could read the disappointment in my face. No one had mentioned Walter but I know both Daniel and Old Joe knew why I was hanging around the bunk house so long.

Wednesday and Thursday my time was taken up with helping a new mother deliver twins. Doctor Johnson was there during the birth and stayed until he was called away to a patient with a bro-ken arm. One of the twins had some difficulty with his breathing. Both the new mother and her husband were very young, seven-teen and nineteen. I felt like an old experienced woman. I took over that household by delegating jobs. The husband's fifteen-year-old sister was there to help the family cope with the newborn.

Two babies were more than they planned for. The breathing of the smallest twin stabilized after about three hours.

Leaving that family for me was out of the question. I stayed Wednesday and Thursday day and night. Thursday morning I sent the teenage sister to fetch a woman I knew that worked as a doula. The woman and I had worked together many times during the war and both babies were, then, stable. She loved newborn babies. Twins would really make her happy.

Thursday about noon, I arrived back home. Disheveled was the only way to describe my condition. The dress I had put on three days before looked like I had worn it a month. My apron had red stains, brown stains, and blue stains from the two nights I slept on a shuck mattress on the floor. A shuck mattress was a tick, or mattress cover, filled with shredded corn shucks. If the shucks were shredded thin enough, they could be comfortable. This mattress, however, felt as though they had left the corn cobs in.

My horse knew the way home. Riding in the saddle with my eyes closed and my head down was restful. I was proud of the way my first job as a trained midwife had gone. Mother and twins were in good hands and I was back home ready for a bath, clean clothes, a good meal and a nap.

The hands I saw holding the reins of my horse when I opened my eyes were not Ole Joe's as I expected. They were the new farm hand's hands. He said, "Ma'am, Ole Joe asked me to meet you. He be fixing supper."

I think my heart stopped. He helped me to dismount just as my father would have. Since Monday, I had daydreamed of our meeting. In my dream, my dress would be pretty, my hair combed, my shoulders straight, my smile bright. Perhaps I would have rubbed my cheeks with crushed red rose petals. Instead, I was dirty, tired and hungry. His first sight of me was of a slumped, tired figure on a horse.

I said, "You may take my horse to the barn." My answer was as though I was dismissing a servant. Never, ever had I treated any farm hand as a servant. No one on that farm did, although Mister and Missus Stuart were addressed as Mister and Missus. They treated everyone as equal. I watched his back as he went to the barn with my horse. His movements were so like my father's I almost cried.

I did get my bath, my clean clothes, my meal and retired to my room for my nap. Sleep did not come. I reviewed my scene with Walter over and over. I thought about how I looked, what I said, how I acted, how I would apologize to him. I was so restless sometimes I lay on my bed, sometimes sat on the side of the bed with my head in my hands. I called myself stupid, stupid, stupid.

When I joined the family for supper, I had calmed down a little. Daniel and I played chess until it was time for Bible reading and prayers. Before Daniel left for Philadelphia, our chess games were very competitive. His father and my father had taught both of us how to play.

That night, Daniel won the game in a very short while. He said, "Cleo, your mind is not on the game. What are you thinking about?"

I lied and said, "I am concerned about the care the twins are getting. The mother and father are so young and the fifteen-year-old sister seemed to be lost in a dream world." I choose not to mention the doula that had come to stay with the twins' family.

During the night I decided to pretend Walter had not seen me arrive the day before. Early the next day, I washed my hair and used a vinegar rinse to bring out the shine. My hair had always been my "crowning glory" and my father was so proud of it. Until he left for Mississippi he did most all the grooming of my hair. In my prettiest day dress, my cheeks and lips brushed with red rose petals, I did look my best.

Watching out the window, I saw Ole Joe and Walter standing in front of the bunk house. Daniel always seemed available to do anything I wanted to do. I said, "I want to tell Ole Joe about the new baby twins. Come go with me."

Daniel was not at all pleased to see Walter standing with Ole

Joe. As we approached the two men, he caught my hand and held it as though I belonged to him.

Ole Joe, ever a gallant man, said, "Cleo, you look like a ray of sunshine."

I almost kissed him. He seemed to have forgotten I had met Walter the day before and introduced us. "Cleo Lamb, may I present Walter Andrews."

I gave a small curtsey and extended my right hand. Daniel was slow in releasing my hand.

Walter hesitated a moment before he took it. As he took my hand and lifted his eyes to my face, he blinked and appeared startled. His handshake was firm but brief. He said, "Howdy do ma'am."

I wanted everyone else to leave. I wanted to have this man that looked and acted like my father to myself. Instead I said, "We are pleased to have you working on the Stuart farm."

No one else said a word for a moment. I started talking about the twins I helped deliver four days before. Walter turned as though he was going to the barn. I said, "Mister Andrews, I would like to have a close up look at your saddle. I have never seen one like it."

Daniel turned slowly around and walked back to the house. Ole Joe went into the bunk house. I was alone with the man whose back I had fallen in love with. We walked to the barn together. He held the tack room door open for me to enter. Looking into the barn, I was not surprised his horse was in the same stall my father's horse had been.

In the tack room his saddle and other gear was in the same place as my father's had been. His saddle and other gear were covered with a red dust cloth. Walter removed the cloth and folded it with great care before he laid it on a chair he had first dusted. The saddle was the plainest one I had ever seen.

Walter said, "This is a McClellan saddle designed by a northern general. The slit down the middle is more comfortable for long rides. It allows air to circulate which cools both the rider and the horse. A soldier does not use a rope so there is no horn. The soldier puts only the toe of his boot in the stirrup to make dismounting easier. This saddle is lighter than the saddles most people use so it can be carried easier." He paused.

I felt he had said this same thing many times. People always asked questions when they saw something different. I looked around the inside of the barn. It looked neater. Tools hung on the walls. Where boards had been missing there were new ones. The stalls were clean. Some of the horses were groomed. They were the horses owned by the Stuarts. Walter's horse was the best groomed of all. Many years before, Daniel had painted a large yellow butterfly on the back wall of the stall in which my horse was kept. That stall looked as though it had been washed down with a brush. The butterfly seemed to glow. Even the center of the barn had been raked.

After we left the tack room, Walter said very little. As usual, I talked, preened, perhaps I whirled a few times. I knew this man was my man. Truly, at that time it did not even cross my mind that he might be married.

Walter still had a dust cloth in his hand when we left the barn. We had just stepped outside when he knelt at my feet and dusted off my shoes. I wrote Iona later, "I had him on his knees at my feet fifteen minutes after I met him."

I ran all the way to the house. After dinner—our "dinner" was in the middle of the day—I went into a cleaning frenzy. My room was always neat but I went over it again and took everything out of the drawers and refolded the clothes. I emptied Father's trunk along with the chest Ole Joe and Daniel had made for me years before. Memories played in my head as I returned things to the trunk. The scarf father's mother had given him when he left Scotland as well as the green stone from her. The chess board and men from the Greek nuns. Lots of bits and pieces from my life and my father's life. The butterflies, a single star. The green silk with the Greek key border I had received as a Christmas present from my father after his death. This I had folded with a layer of homespun. Three or four times a year I took it out and refolded it. This cloth was my most prized possession—even more precious than my beautiful oak chest with the carving of Cleopatra sailing past the oak tree.

Later that day I decided Ole Joe needed my help getting supper for the hands. Missus Stuart and Daniel looked worried. I said, "Ole Joe looks tired. I am going to help him get supper."

Since Missus Bell had moved to the West with Jed, if I was home, I helped with the meals for the family.

Daniel said, "Cleo, I will go with you to the bunk house. We can both help Ole Joe."

He caught my hand as we stepped off the back steps and held it as we walked toward the bunk house. All the farm hands were outside waiting for Ole Joe to ring the bell to let them know the meal was ready to be served. Only when the bell rang did Daniel release my hand.

I went and stood by Walter. I wanted to touch him, rub my hands on his chest, the back of his beautiful neck, his shoulders, his waist, his legs. I wanted to wrap my arms around him. Daniel looked at me as though he understood, then he said to Walter, "Walter are you married or have you ever been married?"

I held my breath and prayed, "Please God let him say no." My prayers were answered.

Walter said, "No."

I was so relieved at his answer my joy must have been revealed in my face. Daniel took one look at me, turned around and went to the barn. We saw him saddle his horse and ride down the lane.

The next two days I hung around the site of the hired hands' house that was being built. Walter could hardly do his work without me being in his way. He did not often look at me directly, just saying, "'Scuse me, Ma'am," once in a while. The other men working on the house found a lot to laugh about. Unrequited love was not funny to the one it happened to. I was both happy and unhappy.

Daniel and his mother and father spent a lot of time together those two days. Before Bible reading and prayers the second night, Daniel asked me to meet him in the parlor early. After we were seated, he said, "Cleo, my plans have changed. I will not be using those two upstairs rooms for a studio."

Somehow I knew what he was going to say. He continued, "No, I have not been to your magic circle to ask for direction for my life. Tomorrow I will be leaving for Philadelphia. In seven days, I sail for France. In the south of Paris there is a colony of artists. Two of my friends are already there. There seems to be nothing here for me."

My thoughts had been so much on Walter I had almost forgotten about Daniel. I cried. He did not cry, he just patted my hand while I cried.

He took my hand and pulled me to my feet saying, "Please, Cleo, do not come to the train station tomorrow. Let me say goodbye to you now."

We hugged each other a long tight hug. The love I felt for Daniel was warm and soft. He was part of my family, he was my past. I knew Walter would be my future. There was no Bible reading for me that night, but there was a long private prayer in which I asked God to help me capture Walter.

It took me seventeen long days, but on the seventeenth day he touched me. I had followed him into the barn. He stopped short, turned around, reached up and stroked my hair. He said, "Child, you just have to find something else to do besides follow me about. The boys are all talking about us."

I was sure the spot on my head he had touched was shining. I stood as straight as I could, looked him in the eyes and said, "Walter, I am not a child. I am nineteen years old, make my own money, and I love you."

He did not seem surprised that I had declared my love for him. He took me into his arms, holding me close as my father would have. I wanted that hug to be a lover's embrace, I felt it almost was.

Then Walter said, "Cleo, the love you feel for me is for a man that is not here. I am a poor hired hand who quit school before he was twelve. That was eighteen years ago. Most of my wages go to my mama in Kentucky. I don't near talk as good as you. Mister Stuart is gonna send me packing if you and me don't straighten this thing out."

The warmth of his body and the beat of his heart told me that he wanted me. I stayed in his embrace as he continued, "Child, the first hour after I rode into Arcidia looking for John Tugman, Mister Stonewall came toward me with his hand extended saying, 'You must be Alexander's brother from Scotland.' Me, not knowing who Alexander was, shook his hand and said, 'No, my name is Walter Andrews. I'm from Kentucky and my brother's name be Willy.' Early on I found out who Alexander Lamb was. Even after almost ten years, he is spoken of with respect. I may look a lot like him, but that is all. I can never be the man he was."

With my head still held tight against his chest, I knew this was my big chance. If I could win him over now, he would be mine. I reached up, put my hands behind his head, pulled his head down until our lips met. The kiss we exchanged was not as a father to daughter but as lover to lover.

Chapter 15

*T*he next Sunday, I went with him to his church. Wanting to make a good impression, I wore my very best Sunday dress, my best hat, my best shoes. I even impressed myself. That was a mistake. The women and men in the church were very plainly dressed. Their clothes were clean and their shoes polished but unadorned. They treated me like a visitor from China. Reverend John Tugman welcomed me as Walter's guest.

The people were kind but distant. For once I was shy. My clothes were not right. I did not know the words to the songs they sang and there was no organ to help me with the music. I was uncomfortable.

The inside of the church was plain. The ceiling was not as high as the Lutheran Church in town. White paint was used on most everything including the pews, except the floors. The floors were natural wood with a wax coating. There was a bright green trim painted around the windows and doors. On the pews were bright colored quilted square pillows. Each square had some of the same shade of green as the window trim. I was told by the song leader that those pillows had been made by the local church ladies, not just by the Baptist women.

After church the people of the congregation stood back not talking and watched Walter and me walk to our buggy. No one left the church until after we did, as though we had been the guests of honor.

By that Sunday everyone on the farm and most of the people in town knew I had chosen the man I wanted to marry. Both Walter and I had talked separately with Mister and Missus Stuart. They gave their blessings. One thing I did not want to do was leave the Stuart farm. I suggested to Mister Stuart that Walter and I could move into the new hired hands' house that was being built.

Mister Stuart said, "Cleo, you know I have promised that place to the hand I hired six months ago. His wife and two children are staying with her mother, who really has no room for them, until this house is finished. I must keep my word. There are fifty acres that includes the woods with your circle and the big oak tree. I will give you that land and help you build a house on it."

"No," I said. "That is too much. I have money, all that money you and our banker tell me about twice a year. I want to spend it. I just want ten acres that includes the oak tree and circle. Our house is to be built on the cleared side of the property that will join your land."

Mister Stuart smiled. I think he knew in advance that would be my reaction. He said, "I told Walter when he asked for your hand in marriage the only way he would get my blessing was if he would accept the gift of a house and land."

I said, "No, I want to pay for this myself."

He replied, "Perhaps he would like this arrangement better."

"Yes," I answered. "He called it 'accepting charity,' and insisted that after we are married we will live on what he earns minus one third that he felt he must sent to his mother." I did remind him of my work as a midwife. I either get paid in cash or services, sometimes a load of wood or hay, sometimes vegetables. When I help Doctor Johnson he pays me in cash. He said, "You can save that money or buy extra fancy things you want."

When Mister Stuart started something, it developed fast. He was as impatient as I. By bedtime that same day we had the plans drawn for my new house. Walter always called it "my wife's house." I got tired of saying "our house" so I would hug him and say "my house."

From the bottom drawer of his desk, Mister Stuart took out a large folder that contained at least twenty house plans. He said, "Cleo, here is your chance. We will build your dream house."

I said, "Let us wait until after dinner before Bible reading so everyone including Walter and Ole Joe can be here. I have a house plan that I drew years ago that is my dream house."

⊷⇒◯⇐⊶

My house plans were very simple. They duplicated the hired man's house my father and I moved into when we came to the Stuart farm. That house had welcomed a nine-year-old girl that needed a home. Father and I lived there through spring, summer, fall and early winter in the year eighteen hundred and fifty-eight. Then I moved into the Stuarts' home and father left for Mississippi, never to return. I wanted to feel the same welcome and love in the new house I would share with Walter.

When we were all seated, I presented my plans. "These plans are like the original cabin built on this farm with a great room that includes a kitchen and living area with bunk beds, three small bedrooms and most important, a porch all around the house." I continued, "Rosa and I had so much fun running around and around that porch. I want my children to feel that same joy."

Everyone was quiet. Then Missus Stuart took a clean page and started sketching. The sketch she made was of a house at least three times larger than the one I drew. While she drew, she asked, "How many children do you want?"

Walter nodded his head to indicate he wanted me to reply to Missus Stuart. Walter and I had discussed our children and even our grandchildren. We had decided we would put it in God's hands. I picked an apple from a basket of apples on the table we were sitting around. Looking at the apple, I replied, "Man can count the seeds in this apple but only God can count the apples in each seed." I paused, "We will follow God's plan."

Missus Stuart reached over and gave me a hug, laughed and said, "You better build a big house. We were going to have two children and ended up with six. If we allowed it to happen, we would still be having babies." The last thing she sketched was a porch completely circling the house.

Ole Joe said to leave one wall in the dining room for him. Later he would build a china cabinet we would be proud of. It would be for the china Daniel was having made for us.

Work started on our house the next day. The new hired man's house and our house were built at the same time. The word got out in town that Cleo was getting married and needed a house. Men, women and children showed up to work. They said I had been there for them while Doctor Johnson was away during the war. The Lutherans came, the Methodists came, the town's people came. Walter was a late comer to the area but he had dedicated so much time to help John the Baptist build both his home and his church that every Baptist thought it was payback time.

Gifts started coming. When Mister Muller, the owner of the biggest store in town, heard that Walter and I were to be married in Riverside Baptist Church, he asked John the Baptist, "Why don't you have music in your church?"

John answered, "Money. My wife misses the organ in the church we left in Kentucky. She could practice any time."

Three days later an organ was delivered to the church. Mister Muller said, "Cleo and Walter need music when they marry."

We received sheets, blankets and dishes. One bachelor gave us a huge iron pot. He said his family every year took it to the ocean and boiled ocean water and collected their salt supply. Doctor Johnson gave us furniture for our bedroom. One day Doctor Johnson sent a package he said had come to him from New Orleans. It contained two wrapped packages just for me. His instructions were to open the small package first.

I was so excited I wanted to share. I pulled Missus Stuart by the hand all the way to the parlor. The packages were not signed but I knew they were from Missus Putman and Starr. My memory of the night Doctor Johnson and I had spent in Missus Putman's house and helped Starr, one of the girls from the Girl House, deliver her baby boy was often on my mind.

The first package contained three beautiful white handkerchiefs with wide handmade lace. They were the most beautiful handkerchiefs I had ever seen and I knew at once I would tuck one of them into the belt of my dress on my wedding day.

Missus Stuart and I sat with our knees together when I opened the second package. Neither of us could believe what we saw. Red and black silk and lace. When she held it up we could see cut out in places you would not believe. I doubt if the brothel in New Orleans had seen the likes of this. At least it was an undergarment. Missus Stuart and I started laughing so hard we rolled around in our chairs.

I stood up, held it against me and started walking and prancing around like I had seen the girls in the Girl House do. Missus Stuart was so like the eleven-year-old Rosa I knew years before. We giggled as though we were little girls. When she could catch her breath, she said, "Cleo, I double dare you to put it on."

In a flash, I was out of the parlor and in my bedroom.

I entered the parlor singing a song I had heard on a stage in Chicago. I strutted, I bumped, I grinned, using the drapery for a prop. I put on quite a show.

A few years later, D.T. told me he heard his mother and me laughing all the way to the barn. He decided to see what we were enjoying so. As he came onto the front porch he saw me through the window and knew we would not want him to be a part of what we were doing.

Walter and I had been married three months before I put it on for him. He did not laugh, he said, "Cleo, I am shocked. That thing is not decent."

We did not make love for three days. That "thing" ended up in the bottom of my oak chest.

We were married March seventeenth at four o'clock in the Riverside Baptist Church. There were very few personal invitations sent out. I wanted everyone that wanted to to come to my wedding. The church was packed. The windows were opened and even the church yard was filled with people. My dress was so beautiful; the green silk was the same color green as the trim of the church windows. Many brides used white as Queen Victoria did. Father had meant for me to use the silk he sent for my Christmas dress the year he died. That year I had not wanted to celebrate. Somehow that cloth was waiting for my wedding.

Reverend John Tugman asked, "Whoever is giving this woman in marriage, please stand." Mister and Missus Stuart stood, then Ole Joe and Doctor Johnson stood. Reverend Tugman surprised me and said, "Whose ever life this man or this woman has touched in a positive way, please stand."

Everyone in the church stood. Even little kids were pulled to their feet. The people outside let out a loud cheer. A feeling of pleasure went through me at their response. This would never have happened in the Lutheran Church. Baptists enjoyed their religious services. If they agreed with the preacher's words, they let him know with an AMEN.

After our wedding everyone was invited to "dinner on the grounds." Food was placed on tables made with five-foot-wide wire fencing. The wire was reinforced on the ends, turned on its side and attached to two trees using log chains. There was so much food some of the men had to construct another table for the desserts.

Fiddles, banjos, a portable organ and other instruments appeared from the wagons, carts and buggies parked in the grove.

Walter and I heard later that it was morning milking time before some of the people left. Country people spend a lot of time alone so there is a lot of catching up to do when they get together.

Walter and I entered our new home side by side. He said he wanted our main door wide enough to carry his coffin through, and that he wanted to live with me in that same house until he died. He got his wish.

I was nineteen, he was thirty. Death was nowhere near us. We were just beginning to live.

The first night after our wedding, we did not do the sex act, nor the next day, nor the next night, nor the day after that. What

126

we did was a lot of exploring. We kissed, we hugged, we touched. As much as I knew as a midwife about other women's bodies, I knew little about my own and even less about a man's.

The third night was a magical night. He was so gentle. If he was surprised that I was not a virgin, he did not show it. If he had asked, I would have told him about Nathaniel, then I would have asked him how he learned just where to touch a woman and just how much pressure to use to give so much pleasure.

Marriage was so right for us. We fitted together beautifully. The only real surprise for me was how sore my face became. No matter how often a man shaved, there was stubble. I was not like Starr. She seemed to want every man, any man. I only wanted my man. I only wanted Walter. Lovemaking was a joy for both of us.

After a week, we went back to work, he, doing farm work for the Stuarts, me, working with Doctor Johnson. A midwife was not needed often, but since I had returned from Chicago, Doctor Johnson wanted me to go on most of his calls with him. Or I was to stay with a patient. This job paid well and he knew Walter wanted us to live on the income from his work. Really, Walter wanted us to live on two-thirds of his income. The money I made he said was to buy stuff we did not need but that I wanted. He knew about my many investments but would not even talk about spending any of that. Truth is, I felt the same. Except for buying the ten acres from Mister Stuart and building our home, my wants had been few.

One day Mister Stuart even said, "Cleo, since you were ten years old, you have been doing work around this house and farm. I should have paid you as I did the other workers." He continued, "You have also given us your joyful love."

What could I say? His words I treasured all my life. I knew that without the Stuarts in my life, I could have been a "street person." As much as I talk sometimes, I was speechless. His words brought on such a wave of emotion. All I could do was hug him. At once my mind went back to when I was ten years old with no mother and no father. I remembered the physical and emotional

127

embrace this man and his family had given me. With that much love and care, money was not needed.

Each year Mister Stuart developed more of the pasture land into farm land. Where the beef cattle used to roam became rows of pepper, tomato, potato, cucumber, corn—even a beautiful field of sunflowers. We still kept a kitchen garden. This was always referred to as "Missus Bell's Garden." Except for the early spring plowing, Ole Joe and I took care of it. We still planted the same types of plants as years past, saving and drying our own seeds. Everyone seemed to think everything from "Missus Bell's Garden" was sweeter than things from the field.

Did I tell you how neat Walter was? In our house, everything had its place. Chairs were either placed straight with the boards on the floor or directly across from other furniture. Books were in the bookcase. Even the handles on the pots and pans when we were preparing a meal pointed in the same direction. Every morning, Walter was the first one up. After he had the fire going and the coffee made, he would come in our bedroom, remove the covers from me and give me a back rub. This made me feel so special. When the rub was finished, he would lift the tail of my nightgown and give me two small bites on my bottom. He was such a dear husband. Then together we made the bed.

We only had three outside buildings—a spring house, a privy and a small barn. Inside our barn was a wagon, a buggy, saddles and other horse gear, a few tools, and our two horses. We kept no cows, no chickens, no dogs, no cats. There was a pump and a stove in the barn. When Walter came home from work, he curried the horses, dusted the wagon and buggy, swept the barn, took a bath and changed his clothes and shoes. It took me a few days to get used to his routine. I wanted him in the house and in my arms. One day I tried to do his dusting and sweeping before he arrived. He took me in his arms and said, "Please, Cleo, let me do this my way. This is how my father kept his barn. Your father's memory is important to you. My father's memory is important to me."

Walter covered the yard around our house with sand, pure white sand. Every Saturday morning he would sweep the yard, always with the same pattern he used in the barn. This account of his neatness makes our life seem boring. That was not true. My marriage was the most wonderful, beautiful three years of my life.

Our joy was complete when two months later my breasts started changing and I started having morning sickness. The only people we told about the coming baby were Doctor Johnson and Mister and Missus Stuart. Of course, I had to tell Ole Joe. Ole Joe, bless his heart, had been there for me ever since my father and I arrived at the Stuart farm. Every young person would be so lucky to have someone like Ole Joe in their lives. Often a grand-parent can fill this role. We did not tell anyone else because we did not want to be greeted everywhere we went with the question, "When is your baby due?"

One Sunday after church, an angry looking young woman stood so close to me our noses almost touched and said, "Bitch, you stole my boyfriend. Bitch. Bitch. Bitch."

The only boyfriend I had ever had was Walter. I knew she could not be talking about Daniel, she could not have known him. Walter, like my father had been, was not much for talking, but I chattered enough for six people about the sermon, the music, the flowers, the people, always about what the women were wearing. That Sunday I hardly said a word on the way home after church. My anger turned to Walter. I was not civil.

I pouted and sulked the rest of the day. I would not even do our Bible reading, handing the Bible to Walter and saying, "You read it."

He read about two verses and put the Bible down. All day he had been trying to get me to tell him what was wrong. In the middle of the afternoon, he gave up and went to the barn. In my mind's eye, I could see him currying our horses until their hides were sore.

In bed that night I turned my back to him, then started crying.

He forced me to turn toward him, holding me close with my face against his chest. He said, "I am truly, truly sorry. I do not know what I have done to make you unhappy. Please tell me. You are my world."

Between sobs I said, "You don't love me. You love that stuck up woman at the church."

He asked, "Which woman at church?"

Still sobbing I said, "The one that wore that ugly blue dress and always walks with her nose up in the air."

With my face against his chest, I heard him give a tiny chuckle. He said, "Never have I spoken directly to that woman. When I first came to town and Mister Stonewall mistook me for Alexander Lamb's brother, I asked other people who Alexander Lamb was. I needed a job. When Mister Stuart offered me a job, I knew I would meet the daughter of the man who was so much respected." He stopped talking; even that was a long speech for Walter.

I waited but he did not continue. If I had been standing, I would have stomped my foot as I said, "So what has that got to do with the woman in the ugly blue dress? Today she called me a bitch and said you were her boyfriend."

He said, "You know that a number of people, some of them families, moved here from Kentucky after the war. John Tugman had been our preacher. We followed him. The woman in the 'ugly blue dress' was one of those. While we were building Riverside Baptist Church, she was always under foot. Until the men began to tease me, I had not noticed that it was my foot she was under. She was always trying to help me. Handing me boards. Picking up my hammer when I laid it down. She got in my way. Due to my size, I never wanted to work on roofs. On that job I got as high up as I could to get away from that woman."

My sobs turned to laughter. I answered him. "She did exactly the same thing I did to try to catch you, except in my case, I was successful."

He continued, "Every time I was around people, they would talk about either you or your father. My resemblance to him triggered their thoughts. Some of the things I heard about you were that you were beautiful, intelligent and rich. They said you went to that church the rich Yankees attended, that an uncle had died

130

and left you a whole lot of money. They said you went to a fancy school in Chicago."

I was amazed that this man I married could and would talk if given a chance. I said, "What else did they say about me?"

He replied, "They said most every single man in town was your boyfriend or wanted to be. Heading the list was Daniel Stuart, then Doctor Johnson's son Amos, some guy out west named Jed, a Greek from New York and even Doctor Johnson, although he was married. They said that you went riding with him alone in his buggy and sometimes you didn't come home for three or four days."

I smiled at that but did not comment.

"They said you were going to move to Switzerland, Virginia, Chicago, out west, New Orleans or Mississippi. For sure you were not going to marry a farmer and stay in this area."

I said, "People must not have much of a life themselves if they spend all that time talking about me."

His last statement that night was, "Three old farm boys even told me they had seen you come out of the Girl House."

He knew I went to the Girl House with Doctor Johnson, so I made no reply. We soon fitted our bodies together like spoons and went to sleep.

Being pregnant gave me a better idea of what women great with child go through. Some moments they feel so ugly, that no one loves them, they want to hide or die. The next moment they glow. After my mood swing the Sunday before and the night time talk with Walter, I became a better midwife. Instead of the non-stop talking I had been doing, I started listening. About-to-be and new mothers need to talk about what they are going through. During labor you would be surprised at some of the things they say. Quite often they express hate for the man that caused them all that pain. After the delivery the hate was usually no longer there and most of the pain was forgotten. God has a way of making new mothers feel blessed.

Chapter 16

"Soft time" was what I called the time Walter and I spent in bed at night after making love. Sometimes during "soft time," I would talk. If I was quiet, Walter would talk. My stomach had just begun to become a little rounded with the coming baby and my world seemed perfect.

During soft time one night, Walter told me about his childhood. His story was very interesting and it made me better understand his obsessions about neatness. He started off by saying, "Papa was an only child. Grandpa and Grandma were a very loving couple both to each other and to Papa and everyone with whom they came in contact. When Papa was about three, Grandpa came home to the farm with a handicapped boy he had found abandoned. The people in town said a wagon had passed through in the middle of the night and left him. He had been in town about ten days. People had fed him but no one wanted to give him a home."

I sighed and thought of the plight of some of the children I had seen in Chicago.

"The boy could not speak. His face and hands were misshapen and his arms were abnormally long. He needed love and care. Grandma said she wanted to put her arms around him and to tell him he was God's child, but she had been around farm animals enough to know she had to use a more subtle approach. In time he learned to sit at a table and eat almost normally. His mouth was off center and the table was not the right height for

132

his long arms. They judged he was about ten years old and named him Oscar. Papa did not remember a time when Oscar was not a member of his family. Oscar became a large man that was protective of Papa and Grandma."

I knew I could not sleep until I had heard more of Walter's story so I encouraged him to continue.

"When Papa was eighteen, he and Grandpa started building a hired man's house on the farm. Before it was finished, Papa met Mama at a hoedown. Papa could play the fiddle pretty good but mostly he liked to dance. I guess he was pretty wild both on and off the dance floor. But to Grandma and Grandpa, nothing was too good for their only child. So when he wanted to marry a girl he had just met, they finished the house they had started for the hired man and the newly married couple moved in. Papa was six feet tall but very thin. Mama was big for a twenty year old and taller than Papa. The farm was still registered in Grandpa and Grandma's names. Everyone knew the whole farm would belong to Papa after they died. Their early married life may have been happy. They had three children in three years. I was born first, then my sister Charlotte and Cora eleven months later. Sometimes my parents would fight and I even saw my Mama hit Papa a few times. Mama always won whatever argument they had. He would retreat to the barn. Things were not too bad until my ninth year. That year Mama 'got religion.'

"We had attended the Baptist Church that Papa's grandfather had helped organize. Papa, my sisters and I continued to go to church with Grandma, Grandpa and Oscar. Two men and two women opened a small store in an empty shack two miles from our house. Soon they were calling it a church. Mama started going three or four days a week to that church, staying most of the day and sometimes she would leave the house at night and not get home until midday the next day. She was always hard to please, but then things got worse. If she was not at 'church' she was either reading her Bible or some secret books she would not let anyone see. Her bedroom door was not only closed but locked.

Sometimes we could hear her praying out loud, maybe not praying, more like chanting.

"Papa first started sleeping in the kitchen, then fixed up a comfortable place in the barn. He was very neat. He not only worked with his father and Oscar on the farm but did most of the house work also. Charlotte and I pitched in some. Cora was more like Mama. We began to notice Mama was getting bigger around the stomach. In due time, my brother William, Willy, was born. I was nine, Charlotte eight, Cora seven.

"Four of the women from Mama's church came to help with the delivery. They looked weird. Their clothes were like none we had seen before and they were noisy. Each one seemed to have her own chant. They chanted so loud we did not hear Mama's birthing screams.

"The women stayed for four days. The first night after they left, Papa, my sisters and I were having our Bible reading in the parlor. We heard the new baby crying. Mama came out of her bedroom holding Willy by one arm. Blood was dripping from his face—he was no longer crying. Mama was yelling, 'Here, you take this God damn thing. He is a devil's child. He ain't yours but you take him anyway.'

"Shock. None of us could believe what we were seeing. Papa was the first to react. When he got close to Mama, she threw the baby at him. He caught Willy, looked around and grabbed an old sweater off the back of one of the chairs. He wrapped the baby as he ran out the door. Charlotte, Cora and I were right behind him. Mama was out of control.

"We all went over to Grandma's house. Willy never came home again. Grandpa and I went to get the doctor. Willy's arm was pulled out of the socket. The blood had been coming from his nose. By the time the doctor had finished setting his arm, Willy was crying.

"I was surprised at the smiles that came over the adult faces when the baby started crying. To me, a crying baby meant trouble. To them it meant the baby was no longer in shock. Grandpa took my sisters and me out on the porch. He had a Bible. He made us swear we would not ever talk about that night, even among ourselves. Cleo, you are the first one I have ever told. To this day, Willy does not know this story.

"Grandma raised Willy and he became a healthy, happy boy. First my sisters, Papa and I moved into our barn. Then, except for Papa, we went back into the house. Mama said she missed us. What she really missed was the cooking and cleaning we did. She did stop going to her church.

"While we were still sleeping in the barn with Papa late one night —I remember there was a full moon—we heard chanting. There were eight to ten people on the porch of our house chanting,'We want our baby. We want our baby. We want our baby.'

"We saw Mama go out on the porch and talk to them. We watched after they left and saw Mama dressed in black come out of the house. She did not see us watching from the barn. She seemed to be sneaking over to Grandma's house.

"Papa said, 'You children stay here and be quiet.'

"He went back into the barn and got a pitch fork. He knew he was not strong enough to fight Mama alone. Before he got past our house, we heard Mama screaming. Oscar had been between her and the baby she was after. When Papa got to her, he did not need the pitch fork. Her legs were full of cuts and she had a badly sprained ankle.

"Between sobs she said, 'That big crazy giant tried to kill me.'

"I am sure Oscar did not touch her, but I am also sure he would have killed her to protect Grandma's Willy. I think Mama got so frightened when she saw Oscar between the houses, that she fell into one of Grandma's rose bushes.

"That night the old building that was called a store—or a church—burned. The four people who lived there disappeared. One neighbor that lived near said he thought he heard a wagon go by his place about three o'clock in the morning. It was not until he got up at five o'clock to start a fire in his stove that he saw lots of smoke coming from the direction of the store. When he saw what was burning, he did not even go near. He told his wife, 'Let it burn. There is not a thing there I would go across the road to save. Not even the people.'

"Mama's 'church' was gone. She did not start going to the Baptist church for many years.

"Grandma would not let Willy come near our house and Oscar made sure her wishes were carried out. Papa, Charlotte and I spent a lot of our spare time with Willy. Mama must have washed him out of her mind. She never spoke to him or about him. Charlotte and I had our house work, farm work and school that kept us busy but we did find time to spend with Grandma's family. Cora did not do much house or farm work. She did attend school. Cora stayed in the house with Mama a lot but each in their own little worlds. I think they spent their time lying in bed, doing nothing.

"When I was twelve, Mama forced Papa to take a job she had arranged at a saw mill. He was a good man but a weak one. He could not stand up for himself or me. Mama also forced me to leave school and do the farm work Papa had been doing. He brought his pay envelope home, unopened every pay day. What she did with the money, I do not know.

"Due to our grandparents, we did not go hungry and we always had clothes. Grandpa took us to town and bought us shoes, underwear, coats, socks, jackets and pants for me and dresses for the girls. The girls had Sunday dresses, shoes and hats. I had a Sunday suit and shoes that I polished three or four times a week just to wear on Sunday. We may have been poor but we were proud.

"Papa had been working at the saw mill a year. I went with him to work a few times. He seemed to be a different person at work. He joked with the men. Once he got in a wrestling match with a man he had been in school with years before. Nobody won or lost, they were just playing around. Sometimes at lunch the boss man would play his fiddle and some of the men would dance. Papa was the best dancer of all. I saw a little of the person my father had been before he met my mother. What God was thinking when he brought those two together, I do not know. Perhaps his plan had to do with the little one we created and you are carrying in that beautiful belly of yours, Cleo."

Then he said, "We need to get some sleep. I will tell you more about my father another time. What next I have to tell is sad."

The next morning Walter held me close and said, "At last I am talking to someone about my father. I feel like a burden is being lifted from my heart."

When he returned from working at the Stuart farm the next evening, we could not wait to get our hands, mouths and bodies on each other. We did not even make it to the bed; a rug was soft enough for us. We found each other in ways we had never dreamed of before. The feeling we both had that evening was what the Bible called "lust." I realized it was what Starr from the Girl House must have felt many times but it was new to me. I only felt it with one man, Walter.

The bread I was baking for supper got so hard we could have used it for a door stop. Instead we put it in our food scrap pail for the Stuart's chickens.

Later, in bed, we made love again. This was a slower, softer kind of lovemaking but so satisfying.

During our soft time I expected Walter to continue his story of his father. Instead he said, "Cleo, this is your time to talk. Another night I will tell you what happened to Papa."

I turned on my back, put my hands under my head and said, "What do you want me to talk about?"

He answered, "Tell me how you got so strikingly beautiful that every eye, man's and woman's, is on you when you walk into a room?"

I did not believe what he said but his saying it made me feel special. I giggled like a ten year old. "My father said my hair was like my mother's. He very seldom spoke of her. He told me how she died and that she was a policeman's daughter from New York. I know that was one of the reasons we moved so often. He was sure my mother's family would take me away from him. Until we moved to the Stuart farm, I would often daydream about Father and I living with my mother's family. The day we arrived here, I knew I was home."

Walter put his arms under his head just as I had done and said, "Tell me more."

A lot of my past I had already told him so I said, "Your nose and my nose are shaped the same. I got my nose from my father. Where did you get your nose?"

He laughed and said, "From my Grandpa Andrews, but tonight we are talking about you. How did you learn to stand, walk and talk like such a sophisticated lady?"

I answered him, "One day, the summer my father and I moved here, Rosa and I were wrestling in the grass. Our dresses were stained and dirty and at times up over our heads. Missus Bell and Missus Stuart were watching us and laughing with us. We heard Missus Stuart say, 'I think it is time I taught those two children how to be ladies.'

"We stood up, ran over to her and Rosa said, 'Mother, we want to be ladies, just like you.'

"Missus Bell said, 'Careful, children, what you ask for. She will teach you to be a Southern Lady. Remember, she is from Virginia and a graduate of Missus Howard's Finishing School.'

"So started our lessons. 'Stand up as tall and as straight as you can, feet flat, no tip toes. Put both hands as high and a straight up as you can, reach for the sky. Girls, quit giggling and watch Missus Bell and I. Our hands and arms are up above our heads. We will lower our arms until our forearms are tight against our sides. Our shoulders will remain in the position they were in when our hands were high above our heads. Try it.'

"We decided trying to be a lady was more fun than wrestling.

"'Now put one foot directly in front of the other, toes pointed forward. Do not bend your knees, take a step, forearms tight against your side with elbows bent slightly. Keep your shoulders in the same position they were in when your hands were above your head.'

We tried it and almost fell sideways. After we quit staggering, she put a book on our heads. We must have been a crazy sight but it was fun. She made us practice, practice, practice. One day the walk became natural to us. James followed us around mocking us. We thought he was being silly with the mimicking he did.

"That summer Rosa and I learned to be 'ladies,' Rosa was eleven. I was ten but we both loved the extra attention we received from Missus Stuart and Missus Bell.

"One day Missus Stuart said, 'Today is the day for you young ladies to learn to flirt.' She handed each of us a fan and had us stand in front of a mirror. She said, 'Ladies no longer use a fan to conceal their smiles, but it is a good tool to use in learning to use your eyes.' We put the fan over the lower part of our faces and started blinking and winking. She taught us how to speak with our eyes.

"Walter, I used some of her tricks on you. I bet you would not have noticed me if I had not flirted with you."

I did not give him a chance to say a word. I continued, "Then she taught us to smile. She said, 'Smiles will get you more than tears.' She was not really teaching us how to flirt with boys. What she wanted us to learn was the correct Southern way to talk to anyone. For me, it worked.

The other day I got an old grandpa that sat on one of my new mother's porches and spit tobacco juice through the rail to use a spittoon. First I put him to work scrubbing the porch and rail. Then I had him go to the woods and dig up two wild rhododendron bushes and plant on either side of the steps. One was right where his tobacco juice had landed for years. I hope it lives.

"While he was busy, I found an empty can, about four inches wide. I put a small amount of straw in the bottom so his sputum would not splatter and put it by his chair. He held his hands behind his back as though he did not want me to see them. They were red, almost blistered. He had used too much hard lye soap and not enough water to clean the porch.

"The job was done. I did not tell him what mistake he had

made. I handed him a can of lard and told him to put that on his hands and told him to use the can I had fixed to spit his tobacco juice in. He was a sweet but tired old man.

"One other thing Missus Stuart had me learn were table manners. She said, 'Cleo, Rosa has used good table manners since she was a child. It would be better if you learned from her.'

"I knew that would mean I would eat more meals with the Stuarts. I turned one of my new 'eye smiles' on Missus Stuart and said, 'I will be delighted.'

"She spoiled the moment by saying, 'You use your knife and fork like your dear father.'

"I froze. A pain shot down my spine, not because she had criticized my father—to me he could do no wrong—but because she called him 'dear.' The last woman I had heard call him dear was the shopkeeper's daughter in the last town we had lived before leaving for the cave where we had spent the winter before. I wanted to say to Missus Stuart, 'Please, please do not call him dear. I want us to stay here with you always.'

The last thing I said to Walter that night was, "Now you know how I got so strikingly beautiful. I think what I do is manipulate."

Walter was so sleepy but I heard him say to himself, "Manipulate. I don't even know what that is."

The next two days and nights were spent with a patient. She had a long period of labor but not a difficult birth. When I handed her the healthy baby girl, she asked for her husband and said to me, "Fred has something to tell you."

He stood with the baby in his arms and said, "Missus Andrews, we decided if the baby was a girl, her name would be Cleopatra Frederica Jackson."

I could not help the tears that spilled from my eyes. This young couple had many people important to them, yet they honored me by giving their first child my name. I felt blessed.

Chapter 17

*T*he first night I was home after Cleopatra Frederica Jackson's birth, we were in the middle of making love when Walter whispered, "Am I being manipulated? Are you manipulating me?"

After that, our word for sex was "manipulate." All couples that have been together awhile have their own private sayings. "Manipulated" was ours.

It had been a week since Walter talked during our soft time about his childhood. I put my hands under my head and said, "Tell me the sad thing about your father." Early in our marriage I had learned that if I didn't control my hands, we would be in action again.

Walter continued his story. "By the time I was thirteen, Mama was doing nothing that even looked like work around either the farm or our house. Papa would come in the house after sleeping in the barn, build a fire in the stove and put the coffee pot on. Then he returned to the barn to milk the cow. Charlotte and I would come into the kitchen, dressed for the day, about the same time. We were both glad of that time together. If it was a school or work day, Charlotte would pack lunches for the four of us. Papa, Cora, me and her. She would make biscuits then run around straightening the house. I would fix the rest of our breakfasts and something for Mama's lunch. This I would put in the warming oven.

"We had to be very quiet. If we bumped a chair, dropped a pot lid or made any kind of noise, Mama would come out of her bedroom carrying a leather strap. She did not care where she hit us—head, legs, back. No place was safe. We would try to protect our faces. Otherwise, we just stood there. After that, she would return to bed. Charlotte would wake Cora and help her get dressed.

"When we returned in the evening, there was always something wrong. The biscuits were too hard. We left a chair in the wrong place. Maybe it was something Papa had done or failed to do. Angry was the only mood I ever remember her being in. Cora did not receive the punishment we did. Cora was so much like Mama. We tried to avoid making either of them angry. When we could, we went over to Grandma's house. Charlotte was like Grandma—tiny, pretty, lots of energy and lots of love to give. Oscar's face would light up when she came in the room. Willy's arms would lift up for her to pick him up. When he got too big for her to pick up, he was always ready with a hug.

"Before this period, I remember one day when she was about five, Charlotte picked a large bunch of wildflowers. Queen Anne's lace, goldenrod and two or three other blossoms for Grandma. Grandma was so pleased she danced around the table, hugging Charlotte and singing, 'You are so beautiful, you are so clever, you are so sweet, I love you so.'

"I was only six but I could feel their joy. Going toward home, we decided to pick some wildflowers for Mama. Cleo, can you see two children ages five and six walking in the back door, their arms full of the gold and white flowers? Can you see their smiles as broad as their faces, joy in their hearts after their visit with Grandma?

"Mama was standing, her back toward us. As we entered the kitchen, she turned around and we saw she was eating a piece of cake Papa had made. She took one look at us and reached for her strap. 'What do you God damn bastards mean bringing that dirty mess in here? Are you trying to kill me? Do you want me to sneeze myself to death?'

"We could not ever remember hearing her sneeze. We ran,

carrying our flowers. We were both crying.

"Charlotte said, 'Let's take the flowers back where we found them.'

"We went back to the field and laid each broken stem as close as we could to its mother plant."

I could not help but cry and remember the love and respect I had received from my father and later from Missus Bell, Jed, Ole Joe, the Stuart family and my many school and church friends. "Why did God make my life full of love and yours contain so much hate?"

Walter said, "I had love in my life. Papa, Charlotte, Grandma, Grandpa, Oscar and my church family loved and respected me. Mama's hate changed me. She did not just hate me. She hated everybody and everything. My sister, Cora, had the same attitude as Mama."

Walter held me. I guess I cried myself to sleep.

The next night Walter continued his story. "Some days were happy—days I spent with Father at the saw mill and days I worked with Grandpa and Oscar in the fields. I was big for my age at thirteen and could do a man's work. After working in the field one day with Grandpa and Oscar, I stopped by Grandma's house to wash up.

"Willy was standing with three large fish already dressed for me to take home. 'John Henry'—a neighbor two farms over—'brought Grandma a whole mess of these. She wants you to have some.'

"I picked him up, fish and all and swung him round and round. There was never a happier child than Willy.

"Charlotte had started supper when I arrived home. When Papa got home, everything was ready. Usually Charlotte, Papa and I ate and saved the best for Mama and Cora to eat later. This night they both joined us at the table. After Grace, we started to eat and Mama was almost cheerful. The rest of us were silent, waiting for her to explode in anger.

"Then she said, 'Walter, I have good news for you. Tomorrow

143

you start work at the saw mill.'

"I felt a surge of joy. I would be spending all day working with Papa and getting paid for it. There was a tiny urge to hug Mama, but I sat still and punched Charlotte under the table. She was grinning for she knew how much I wanted to work at the saw mill. I was afraid she would cause Mama to change her mind and start yelling.

"The next morning Mama joined us for breakfast fully dressed, something she had not done for years. While we were eating she said, 'Your Papa is going to take me to Garland to buy me a pair of shoes. Walter, you will have to go to work alone.'

"Papa looked uncomfortable. Garland was half a day's drive away and Mama had always driven herself any place she wanted to go. That was the first work day she had ever allowed him to miss.

"Saw mill work is hard. Those men work hard, play hard. They had fun calling me Baby Walter. The day went fast.

"Arriving home, Mama met me in the yard, appearing very angry, her dress dirty and her hair untidy. She yelled, 'That son-of-a- bitching Papa of yours went off without taking me to Garland.'

"I asked, 'What happened?'

"She answered, 'First he said he had to fill in that old dry well behind the barn. Then this old man I did not know, came by in a wagon and talked to him awhile. He picked up his short pitch fork and left with that old man.'

"I walked behind the barn to the old well which had been dry since before Grandpa and Papa built our house. Papa was careful to keep boards or logs over it so no person or animal would fall into it. He had never talked to me about filling it in. As little children when Charlotte and I learned that China was on the other side of the globe, we would spend time watching for Chinese people to come out of the well. Sometimes we were sure some of the logs moved or had been moved.

"That day when I went to the area, I saw the logs and boards had been moved and the well filled. I found Mama and asked her,

'Why, Mama, why was it important for Papa to fill that old well today? It has been there as long as I can remember.'"

Walter quit talking, remembering that day was more than his emotions could bear. He sobbed. When he got control of his emotions, he said, "What I could have done, what I should have done, I don't know. I just stood there while she ranted on about Papa filling the well using dirt and rocks and all sorts of mess to fill up that hole that went all the way to China. She also said, 'He better be here to milk that old cow tonight or I'll get my leather strap to him.'

"I turned and went to the barn. The barn was neat and orderly, just as Papa always kept it. Except the pattern the broom made on the dirt floor was different. It did not have the slight curve Papa liked to make. His short handle pitch fork was missing from the wall. Two shovels, a square headed one and a round headed one had been washed but were still streaked with dried mud. Papa was always careful with all his tools. He oiled them every time he used them.

"Mama came into the barn behind me, picked up the broom and started sweeping, all the time cussing and fussing, 'That son of a bitch wouldn't take me to Garland to buy new shoes. He better be here to milk the cow.'

"I left her raving and went into the house to start supper. Charlotte and Cora came home from school and Mama repeated the tale she had been telling since I got home from the saw mill.

"Papa did not come home to milk the cow and he was not there the next morning to build a fire in the stove. No neighbors heard the wagon Mama said he went away in. Charlotte and I did the chores he usually did. I went to work, the girls went to school. For three days Mama did a little around the house. Then she went back to her old habits, angry as ever with her leather strap nearby."

Walter was quiet for a few minutes. So was I, somehow I knew it would be better if I let him mentally relive that time in his life.

He continued, "Saturday was pay day. Mama told me to have

my pay put in a sealed envelope, just as Papa had and bring the envelope to her unopened. When the boss handed me the envelope, he included on the outside two bills. He smiled and said, 'Us men have to have some secrets.'

"That was the first time I remembered Papa had pointed out to me a place in the barn loft and said, 'Behind that board is something your Mama doesn't know about.'

"I added my two bills to the money in the barn loft Papa had saved and did that for the next two years. When I was fifteen, the saw mill moved to the other side of Garland. Mama was mad but the timber was cleared out and they had to move. I went with them and lived in the lumber camp with the other men in the crew. The first Saturday I came home to give Mama my pay envelope.

"Charlotte met me in the barn and said, 'Walter, I can't take it anymore. I am leaving in the morning. Nobody can live with Mama and do all the chores, cooking, cleaning and what else she can yell about.'

"I was not surprised. I asked, 'Where will you go?'

"'Miss Watson'—her teacher—'said I could sleep on a cot in her room until she could find some other place for me. Somehow Cora found out my plans and said if I did not let her go with me, she was going to tell Mama. I wanted to see you one more time before we left.'

"I gave her all the money Papa and I had saved. He was not coming back. In my heart, I felt he was in the bottom of that old well with a pitch fork in his back."

After what Walter called his "confession," he was more relaxed. He was still as neat as ever. The barn was swept, no blade of grass dared to grow in the sand-covered yard that completely surrounded the house. Handles on cups, pans, and pots in the kitchen were pointed in the same direction as were spouts on kettles and tea pots. Early in our marriage, I teased him about his neatness. I found myself conforming and began to appreciate the order small touches made.

One night during our soft time, I said, "What happened to your sisters and what were your grandparents doing during the time you talked about the other night?"

This time he held me while he talked. "Cora was back home with Mama when I brought my pay envelope home the next Saturday night. I asked Cora about Charlotte but Mama broke in cussing and yelling about how 'that whore took off with some man headed for some God forsaken place she never heard of.' Cora ran into her room and shut the door.

"I went to the barn; it was a mess. The cow's milk bag was so full and her tits were covered with sores. There must have been no milking done since Charlotte left. It took me a long time, but I milked the cow, carefully because of the sores. There was some pus and also blood in the milk but the cow was more comfortable. The next morning I milked her again then took her to the man that was renting Grandpa's farm and told him he could have the cow if he would put a quart of milk in Mama's spring house every day and two pounds of butter once a week. He was not very interested in having a cow with sore tits but said he would keep her until he talked to Willy.

"Later that Sunday I went to talk to Charlotte's teacher, Miss Watson. She told me my sister had gone west with a family she knew that had two small children. Charlotte was to pay for her trip by helping care for the children. Cora had said she did not want any part of caring for a bunch of snotty-nose kids and was going home to Mama.

"If Charlotte ever wrote home, I was never told. Miss Watson got a letter from her friends my sister left with. The letter said they were going to stay a while in a town on the Mississippi but sent no return address. I knew Charlotte well enough to feel she would land on her feet and that she had not spent the money I gave her.

"Grandpa did not last long after Papa disappeared. He seemed to lose his will to live. In two months, he went from a healthy, robust farmer to a thin rake of a man. He rented his farm to his hired man, Mister Jenkins, after he laid off a three acre square that included Mama's house. The renter was not to farm that. Grandpa moved his family, Grandma, Willy and Oscar to my Great Aunt Lula's house in town. Aunt Lula—Grandma's sister—never married and still lived in the house their parents owned.

"Grandpa died a month later. Grandma and Oscar lived two years more. When Grandma was in her casket, Willy put a white rose in her folded hands. Two weeks later they found Oscar dead in his bed with his hands folded over a small bunch of queen-Anne's lace, roots and all.

"Each week I had been sending Mama most of the money I made. I did not visit our farm but went often to stay overnight at Aunt Lula's house. Grandma had the lifetime rights to the farm, then it was supposed to go to the male heirs. One Monday I stayed over and we went to the courthouse and I signed over my share of the farm to Willy.

"When I left, Willy was a man with a tiny beautiful wife named Rachel and two children. You could hardly see Mama's house for the weeds and bushes. There was a path that went through the brush to Mama's spring house. Willy's wife told me the renter, Mister Jenken, left two quarts of milk a day and two pounds of butter a week, also two dozen eggs. I guess all Mama's hens either died or were eaten.

"Rachel and Willy stopped by Mister Jenken's house every Sunday after church and left a basket. They picked up the empty basket by an old milk can Missus Jenken kept her chicken feed in and someone took it over to the spring house when they delivered the milk. Rachel packed the basket with food, some she canned herself and some she bought from the store. Willy ran the store that Rachel's father started.

"Willy went to college for two years and became a teacher. He only taught one year before getting a summer job in Rachel's father's store. He then married the store owner's daughter and lived happily ever after. He was such a joy to be around. What Grandma and Grandpa told him about Mama, I do not know.

Rachel said he talked a lot about growing up on the farm, a lot about Grandma, Grandpa, Oscar, Charlotte and me, but he had never spoken to her about Mama or Cora."

I said, "Let us leave your mama alone and not even think of her and Cora anymore."

One day I did ask him if he was sure his mother received the money he sent every month.

"Yes, a couple of years after I joined the Confederate army, it was late. We had marched all day. Everyone was tired and ready to settle down for the night. A very young soldier came up to me and said, 'I know you. We used to go to the same church. You are Walter Andrews.' He continued, 'Your Mama said if I ever saw you to tell you to send her more money, that Cora was eating her out of house and home.' He added, 'I'll talk to you tomorrow.' I never saw him again."

Hate for Walter's mother build up in me, then I asked myself, "Am I marking my baby? This woman was his grandmother and Cora his aunt. Will my baby grow up hating people he did not even know?"

It was almost Christmas and I called myself a Christian so I decided to try to ease my conscience by doing something nice for her. I made her a dress. A lady at church pointed out another woman she said was Walter's mother's size. The material I selected was mostly black with white and red colors mixed in. I tried to put love into every stitch of that dress.

Walter saw me working and said, "Cleo, what pretty cloth."

I did not tell him it was to be a Christmas present for his mother. Shortly after Christmas, I received a letter from his mother. She wrote:

In the day of our Lord January 1st

In the year of our Lord 1868

To my son Walter's wife,

I take my pen in my hand to write you a letter. This finds me well, hope you are the same.

She went on to tell me all the pains she had—her feet, her

149

back, her stomach— and even the weather was bad. There were two pages about her health. Then, "I burned that package you sent. My fingers did not touch that evil thing. That color has never been allowed in my sight. I even had Cora take the ashes out of the fireplace after I burned it and scatter them in the field."

I did not finish reading that letter. I burned it and almost caused a fire when I put the hot ashes in the field. For two days my mind went blank. Somehow I did my housework but my heart was not in it. When Walter would ask me what was wrong, I answered, "Nothing."

Nightly we went over to the Stuart's house for Bible reading and prayer. I had been the main reader since James' death, sometimes they wanted me to read other than the Bible but we still called it Bible reading even if I read Shakespeare or Greek poetry. That night the poem was about the color of the rainbow. I asked, "What color would you paint evil?"

D.T. said, "Black. I have heard people say 'black as sin.'"

Ole Joe said, "Maybe yellow. Pus is yellow."

The answer I was waiting for came from Walter. "Red. My Mama always said red was the color of evil."

So my question was answered. The small amount of red in the dress I sent his mother made it "evil." The next day I went to town and bought the reddest material I could find. I made a dress for myself and wore it to church. The ladies at church complimented me. No one ever hinted that the color was evil.

My health was excellent. My baby arrived on time. I carried my baby low and was sure it would be a boy. The name I selected was Walter Alexander. Doctor Johnson, Missus Stuart and a midwife were with me when my daughter was born. Husbands were not allowed to witness a birth. Between my contractions, Missus Stuart and I sang Welsh songs Missus Bell had taught us years before. Music did help with pain.

Missus Stuart was the one who caught my baby. She did not tell me if it was a boy or girl. She turned the crying baby around so I could see for myself. Giving birth was tiring. I went to sleep as soon as I delivered the afterbirth. When I awoke, Walter was sitting by my bed with a big smile on his face holding the baby wrapped in a soft white blanket.

He said, "She is like a beautiful white pearl."

I was still groggy and repeated, "White pearl." That is how my daughter got her name. No, she was not named "White Pearl." We named her Pearl Louise. Why Louise? It sounded right.

Chapter 18

*P*earl was an easy baby to care for—too easy. I had to put her on a schedule. Most babies cry when they are hungry and let you know when their diaper needs changing. She slept a lot and made little soft noises. She was the pride of Walter's life. At church he would strut around like he had the prettiest, smartest baby ever born. When we were in the buggy together, I was in charge of the driving. He said it was his job to take care of Pearl.

Ole Joe, Missus Stuart and D.T. also helped with her care.

Pearl was a little slow learning to walk or talk. After she started sitting up, she could entertain herself for hours with a few toys. It was easy for me to read, sew or do housework. When Ole Joe and I would work in Missus Bell's Garden, we put her on a blanket at the gate end of the garden with a few toys and she gave us no trouble. Perhaps I had not wanted a crying baby but I had wanted a baby with more energy than Pearl displayed.

Walter would play with her for hours and maybe get a smile or two but never a laugh and certainly not a giggle. Before she learned to walk, he would run with her in his arms round and round the porch that encircled our house. She seemed to like that. When she started walking, he encouraged her to walk the circle of the porch. She would walk a very short ways and sit down. Never in my lifetime did I see any children of mine use that porch as Rosa and I had when I first came to live on the Stuart farm.

Most of the laughter and giggles in that house were from me during the time I spent in bed with Walter. That was not entire-

152

ly true. We were a happy family but lots of our happy time was spent at the Stuart house. If I was not working with a patient or with Doctor Johnson, most of the time I was gardening, canning, tending the chickens, helping with housework, doing something at the Stuart's. Walter, Pearl and I were always there for Bible reading and prayers. The walking path between the two houses was well worn.

Keeping our house was a snap. Walter got up every morning and made the fire. Then he woke me with a back massage and two bites on my bottom. While I dressed, he made our bed and put the house in order. Not much to that. Maybe a pot handle was pointed the wrong way. He made coffee and fixed fried cakes or porridge, or ham and eggs, always biscuits, while I fed Pearl and got her ready for the day. Twice a week the wife of one of Mister Stuart's hired hands came over and did the washing and ironing. Walter left after breakfast to do farm work.

This system worked well for us. At our house we had no garden, no chickens, no cats. We did have a barn and two horses. Inside the barn were the horses, a few tools, gear, the old wagon that Father had for so many years and a beautiful new buggy. From the Stuart farm we got our milk, butter, eggs, already dressed chickens, and meat from the hogs and cows that were killed for the family. Missus Bell's Garden supplied fresh vegetables. What was not used fresh was canned.

The Stuart farm was a real show place. They trucked corn, cucumbers, beans, tomatoes and other crops by train to Chicago. Mister Stuart was a man for his time. America and the world were changing. If he heard of a new invention, he wanted part of it. He did a lot of traveling—trains made it easy. For a while, he had his own train car but gave it up. He said it was not worth the trouble. Arcidia was growing. He built a tomato cannery, then a pickle factory. The first year he made pickles they spoiled; the vinegar was wrong. So he imported apples and started his own vinegar plant. He called it a "cider mill."

Missus Stuart and D.T. played a large part in his busy life. He

hired a farm manager and plant managers for the other businesses. Ole Joe and Walter were given nice raises in pay and had different things to do most every day. They were told what to do by
Mister Stuart, not by the farm manager. It was a good life.

Doctor Johnson hired a nurse to help him and a full time sec-
retary. He build an addition on his house and called it a clinic.
The clinic included an office for me. There were more people in
town and more babies being born. Sometimes I helped Doctor
Johnson, but most of the time I was busy with my babies.

One day Doctor Johnson said, "Cleo, Dan"—that is what he
called Mister Stuart—"is starting to build a new plant down near
the river. I will be over there if you need me."

I knew about the new plant and also knew Ole Joe and Walter
would be there to help lay out the foundation for the building.

Pearl was a little over two years old and playing happily with
toys in the corner of my office. Doctor Johnson had left the
office about an hour before. I was sitting at my desk reading a
new medical book about cancer and thinking about James, the
Stuarts's son who died when he was ten with cancer. A strange
feeling came over me, a sensation that started in my lower back
and slowly traveled up my spine. It was nothing like I had ever
felt before. When it got to my head, my mouth flew open and I
shouted, "Walter!"

For a minute I was numb, then gathered Pearl up and ran to
the stable shouting, "Bring me my buggy."

The stable hand was fast and had that horse hitched to the
buggy by the time I got Pearl settled.

I did not hit anything or anybody on my wild dash to the
building site. Later I was told I came close to having an accident.

Walter was stretched out on the ground when I arrived. Handing Pearl to the man that stopped my horse, I pushed through the
men gathered around Walter and Doctor Johnson. No one needed to tell me. I knew Walter was dead. When I squatted down
beside him, he still had color in his face. I put my hand over his
heart and felt no beat. No one spoke.

Then I heard a small voice say, "Papa, Papa come on and play with me."

The only man I ever loved had died. That is not quite true. The first man I loved, my father, died when I was ten. Walter had been so like him in many ways—the way he looked and the way he treated me, the way he brushed my hair.

Mister Stuart took my left hand and pulled me to my feet. He gathered me in his arms and just held me. I knew men were removing Walter's body and I heard Doctor Johnson's nurse talking to Pearl. Somehow I got through the next four days. I was told Walter had been coiling a rope they were using to measure the foundation of the new factory. He stood with the rope still in his left hand when he put his right hand over his heart and said, "Oh, my God."

Both Mister Stuart and Doctor Johnson caught him as he fell. When I arrived, the rope was laying by his left side.

Our life together had been good. He was an easy man to live with and to love. He was a better husband than I was a wife. I had moods. Sometimes I was jumping with joy, another time crying or maybe giggling. He was neat, calm and a joy to hold at night.

Four days after Walter's funeral, his brother Willy came to see me. He looked a lot like Walter, not quite as tall but an easy man to like. You could look at the creases around his mouth and tell he smiled and laughed a lot.

That was not a time to laugh.

Willy stayed with us for three days. Pearl and I were staying with the Stuarts; my old bedroom was always ready for me. Willy talked about his childhood with Walter. Walter had been his much loved older brother. He did not speak of his mother but once.

I said to him, "I will continue to send Walter's mother the same amount of money each month he always sent her."

He was surprised. He said, "I did not know Walter was sending that woman money. My wife makes sure she has milk every day and other food stuff every Sunday. Rachel puts money in the basket that the man takes to the spring house. Those two women never lift a hand to do anything."

We talked of other things, his two children, the older boy
named Walter and the younger one named Oscar. He said there
was another one in the oven that he hoped was a girl. If so, one of
her names would be Charlotte.

He spent a lot of time with Ole Joe and Mister Stuart. Most
farmers counted on their farms for income. Mister Stuart could
afford to use his for experiments. Any new farm equipment might
be used. Willy was a storekeeper but very interested in new farm
equipment. When he left, I gave him the saddle Walter brought
home from the war, a MacClellan saddle.

Life went on. Pearl and I stayed nights with the Stuarts for
two weeks, going often to our house. One day, crying, I said to
Ole Joe, "What am I going to do? I can't walk into our house
without seeing Walter."

Ole Joe said, "Go over there and change things. I will help you.
We will move everything around except the stove and the sink."

We did. Pearl and I moved back home. We turned pot handles, turned tea pot spouts all different directions. We moved my
personal things from the bedroom Walter and I had shared into
a smaller bedroom. The bed Walter and I used was put across a
corner. If it could be moved, we moved it. Then we went outside.
Part of the sandy yard Walter had swept every Saturday had been
plowed up for me by one of the farm boys. Ole Joe and I started
an herb garden. We also planted gooseberries, blackberries, rasp-
berries, and blueberries. We even moved the wood pile. We did
leave wide sandy paths that I started sweeping every Saturday.

Pearl was an easy child to ignore. She seemed to feel no joy or
sorrow. The hired man's little girls would come over to play with
her, and they would run round and round the porch of our house,
laughing and giggling, as I had dreamed my children would. Not
Pearl. She sat watching them, not joining in their joy.

Maybe I was not a good mother. I tried. She developed mentally and physically. She could read and write before she went to
school. When she read aloud, her voice was a monotone. If she

sang, you would think she only knew one note. Never was she the "challenge" I had been. In school, she rated below average.

One day shortly after we moved back home, Walter's memory was still fresh but I felt I had made the house mine. A cleaning spell hit me. After I straightened and cleaned the rest of the house, I started on the bedroom Walter and I had shared. The head of the bed was very high. I had to stand on the bed to dust the top. I dropped my dust cloth behind the bed. There was no way to reach it. When Ole Joe came for his daily visit to bring me milk, I asked him to help me move the bed from the corner to where it had been before Walter died. He went back to the Stuart farm and got two farm hands to move the bed.

Ole Joe and I always had a chess game going. We were playing that night until close to midnight. The time we set long before to quit for the time being. He stood up, stretched, looked around as though surprised and said, "Cleo, do you see what I see?"

Walter's ghost had not done it, but the house was back as though Walter had never left. The handles on the frying pans and pots and tea pots were pointed in the same direction. The chairs, rugs, everything was back where it had all been before. Ole Joe teased me and said, "Bring the lamp. Maybe the herbs and berry plants have disappeared."

I had not been aware I was doing it. Habits are habits. Except for minor changes, my house remained the same the rest of my life.

Everyone should have someone like Ole Joe in their lives. From Mister and Missus Stuart I received security and respect. From D.T., I received admiration and almost worship. Walter and my father had given me love. Doctor Johnson gave me a sense of purpose. Ole Joe gave me some of all the above plus serenity. From Pearl I do not know what I received or what I gave. I know I offered everything I had. In the end, I did not even give her security.

Willy's wife Rachel sent me a letter about every six months. She told me about the birth of little Charlotte, what Willy was doing, how sweet her boys were, and what trouble they got into.

No mention of Walter's mother or sisters. Walter had been dead about two years when she wrote that his mother had died. She enclosed the last envelope I had sent his mother unopened. She explained that the day Missus Andrews died, Cora had come to the post office, broke into a conversation the postmaster was having with the mayor's wife, and demanded her mail. He had heard that her mother had died and he knew there were two envelopes addressed to her mother. The same two envelopes had been coming to her for years once a month and he knew they contained money. This time he did not give them to Cora. Cora left the post office very angry.

He sent a boy to the store for Willy. As "head of the family," as the postmaster called Willy, he should be the one to decide what to do with the envelopes. Willy had never spoken a word to his mother or even looked in her direction when he could avoid it. Willy asked the sheriff, the mayor and the mayor's wife, plus his lawyer to witness the opening of the second envelope. The envelope contained only money and a name as address. Missus Hubert Rolle, General Delivery, Shadow, California. Willy knew it had to be from Charlotte.

The next day, he was on the train to California. There was no direct route to Shadow. It took him about a week as part of the trip was by stage. The last part was by train. He asked the station master if he knew Charlotte Andrews. The station master said, "Yes. She has been our school teacher for a long time. Now she is married to Hubert Rolle, a fine young man."

The children had been let out of school to watch the train go by and to wave at the engineer and passengers. The train did not stop unless someone was waiting to get on or off the train. Most of the town was watching when Willy arrived. He walked up to Charlotte standing in the school yard. She held her hand out and shook hands with him saying, "So glad to see you. So glad you came."

He said, "Charlotte" and took her in his arms. The whole town watched.

She stepped away from him, appearing very embarrassed. She

had ordered new slates for the school and thought he was delivering them. He said, "I am Willy, your brother."

"No, no, you can't be. It has been too long." Then it was she that gathered him in her arms with the whole town watching including her husband.

She taught school as she had done since she arrived in Shadow, traveling with a wagon train. She was only sixteen when she arrived but had been a good student in school and brought seven books with her all the way from Kentucky. The town had no school. She started one with those seven books. At first, the town gave her room and board. After six months, they started paying her. At age nineteen, she married the son of Richard Rolle, a local rancher.

Richard had immigrated to the United States from England and loved to tell stories of living in a cave in England. He said he was known as Richard the Hermit. Charlotte told Willy about the money Walter had given her when she left Kentucky. Part was from him and part from some their Papa had hidden under a board in the barn loft. She was proud that she had spent none of that money until after she got married. She had supported herself by taking care of children on the trip to California, then by teaching after she got to Shadow. The money was spent buying a bull and ten breeding cows. That was how she and her husband started their spread. It was growing. They also had two boys. The oldest one was named Walter. It seemed as though everyone could have a boy named Walter except me.

Willy had asked Rachel to write a letter to Charlotte that he would carry to her telling about their mother's death. He said to Rachel, "That dirty old woman's name is not going to pass my lips."

Charlotte read the letter and did not ask about her mother or Cora. She sent a note back to Rachel enclosing the money from the envelope Willy had returned to her plus double the amount. In the letter she asked Rachel to give the money to Cora and tell her there would be no more.

All this information came to me in four different letters from

Rachel. She stated she had put the money in the usual Sunday basket the tenant took to the spring house. She had also put the usual amount of money she had been putting in every fourth basket. Her note to Cora read, "This is all the money you will ever receive from Charlotte or Rachel."

The last few times she had delivered the basket, she had seen a seedy looking man hiding in the brush and she was sure he was staying with Cora. Rachel instructed the tenant to continue with the milk, butter and eggs but that was the last basket of other foods she would be bringing. About three months later, Rachel wrote that no one had been living in that run down shack that Willy owned. They had burned it to the ground, plowed up the dirt and planted corn. I did not tell them that the dry well they plowed over probably contained the remains of Walter's father.

Willy was not the natural son of an Andrews man but was loved as though he was and deserved that love. Rachel and I exchanged Christmas gifts and letters for a few years. Then even that stopped. People either grow closer or farther apart as years pass.

And the years did pass. More people moved into our area. More vegetable farms were started. Mister Stuart's empire grew. The only farming he did was on the original farm and he hired a manager for that. There were always new farm hands on the Stuart farm, mostly young boys. When they had worked there for a while, they were given better paying jobs by Mister Stuart and other young men were hired. Ole Joe and I still tended Missus Bell's Garden and also took care of the chickens. Two of the farm boys were doing the rest of the barn work, milking the cows, tending the horses and so forth.

Ole Joe's job of cooking for the crew was assigned to someone else. He spent a lot of time whittling, carving wood figures of cows, horses, cowboys, whatever he could think of. Missus Stuart took all he would part with to a big store in Chicago. Ole Joe made money that way.

I was busy. Pearl grew. She was not interested in doing much except tending herbs. The herb garden I started after Walter died grew larger and well. We started selling some of the garlic and dill to Mister Stuart's pickle plant. We did not grow near enough for his needs but it did give Pearl an incentive to do something. "Somber" was a word I used to describe Pearl.

In a real way, we had two homes. The path between our house and the Stuart's was well worn. When I worked at the clinic, sometimes Pearl was with me. Other times, she was at the Stuart place and occasionally with the farm manager's family. If she wanted to stay home, Ole Joe came over to our house and did his whittling. I became careless, I know. She liked to wander in the woods alone. That I could appreciate. It was also one of my favorite things to do.

Pearl was twelve and could take care of her own needs. One time I knew I would be gone for three days with midwife duties. As I left, I put a book on the table and told her not to forget to return it to Missus Stuart for me.

My plan was to be with my patient for the birth of her second baby and also to visit with her and her family. There was so much joy in that family; I looked forward to the time I would spend with them. Four generations lived in that big old "ghost house."

I had almost met the ghost two years before when I was there to help with her first baby's birth. In the patient's upstairs bedroom, I opened what I thought was a closet door. It was a door to a very narrow staircase. The staircase was dark, dusty and sealed off at the lower end.

Amy, my patient said, "You have found our ghost."

The house had been built for her husband's great, great grandfather and mother. The bedroom was the one they used. After the great, great grandfather died, his wife had the small narrow staircase built so her husband's ghost could visit her without disturbing the rest of the family. She told the family about his nightly visits. After she died, her son enlarged the house and covered the lower end of the stairs.

Chapter 19

*W*hen I returned home after three days, I found Pearl sitting in a straight wooden chair that we rarely used. She had her best dress on, looking the cleanest I have ever seen her. She was never really dirty, but she did like to wear the drabbest clothes. This dress was a bright blue.

I said, "Sweetheart, you look real pretty." She was never a beauty, but that day she did look pretty to me.

She said, "I am soiled."

Being a midwife, I should have understood, but I didn't. I replied, "Honey, you are not soiled. There is not a spot on that beautiful dress."

She answered, "Mama, I am soiled. A man soiled me."

I could not believe what I was hearing. I said, "Pearl, do you mean you have been raped?"

She hung her head and in a small voice said, "He soiled me."

When Pearl was six, she had overheard Doctor Johnson and me discussing two patients. The woman was pregnant and the man had a sore on his penis. We were wondering what affect syphilis would have on the fetus.

When the doctor left the room, Pearl said to me, "Mama, don't talk dirty."

I said, "I was not talking dirty. I used the proper names for our body parts."

Pearl said, "You were too talking dirty. Yesterday I heard one man say you talked dirty to his wife. Please don't talk dirty or

God won't let you into heaven."

So, around Pearl, my speech patterns changed. "Penis" became "thing," vagina or the pubic area became "down there" or "private parts." First intercourse or rape became "deflowered" or "soiled."

I tried to remain calm as I ran to the stable for my horse and buggy pulling Pearl along with me. Both Doctor Johnson and his nurse were in their offices when the two of us arrived. It took some persuasion, but Pearl finally agreed to let the doctor examine her. I left the room. Pearl said she did not want me to see her "private parts."

After the examination, Doctor Johnson said she had been "deflowered" but no other damage was done except Pearl had done some aggressive washing in her pubic and thigh areas with lye soap. A rash covered the lower part of her body.

I asked the doctor, "Did she tell you who the man was?"

He said, "She said she did not know him and that she did not want to talk to me about it." He also said, "We will not know for a while if she is pregnant. You know I have a 'magic wand' if you want me to use it."

We had used the term magic wand for years, since Starr had used that expression to describe how Missus Putman kept her from getting pregnant while she lived in the Girl House. As a midwife, I never destroyed an embryo.

I told him, "No. If it is God's will for my twelve-year-old daughter to have a baby, he has a reason."

Pearl went to sleep soon after we returned home. The doctor had given her a sedative. She was afraid I would leave her so I lay on the extra bed in her room until I heard Ole Joe and Missus Stuart in the next room. We still had not heard from Pearl how the rape had happened but Missus Stuart heard about it in town and hurried home to be with me. There are no secrets in small towns; words travel fast.

Two hours later, the three of us, Missus Stuart, Ole Joe and I, saw through the open door that Pearl was awake. We were quiet and waited for her to join us. She had changed her dress. She wore one of the drab grey things of which she was so fond. We sat around a small table with cups of herb tea that no one drank. I felt guilty. How could this rape have happened? How could I have prevented it? Who did it? These questions and more went through my mind.

When Pearl came in the room, we all stood. She took a chair by the table and I poured her a cup of tea. We returned to our seats and faced her over the table. This was the story she told.

"Mama, after you left three days ago, I decided before going over to Missus Stuart's to go to your magic circle near the oak tree and ask God for guidance. I wanted Him to show me a butterfly and a ray of sunshine as He did for you after Grandpa Lamb passed on. I wanted some of the joy you have. Before getting to the circle, I had to pee."

Farm women of that era did not wear under-drawers. They wore four or five petticoats. When they had to urinate, they stepped off the path, spread their legs a little, made sure their petticoats would not get wet or their shoes sprinkled and urinated.

Pearl continued, "Before I started to pee, I had looked around to be sure no one was watching. My hands were busy holding my skirt away from the flow. I heard not a sound until a hand was put over my mouth. A voice in my ear said, 'Be quiet. Do not yell. You are going with me.'

"Then a bandana was put over my mouth and my hands were tied. I was not really afraid; I was sure someone was playing a game with me. After all, I was on my way to ask the God of the oak tree to give me direction for entering into womanhood. When I got to look at him, I knew he was a stranger. He was tall and slender, about the size of Uncle D.T., except he was dark. I don't know if he was gypsy or Indian or something else. He was darker than any folks around here. He was also quiet. Mama you are always talking and noisy. The most he ever said was the last day. He led me to that old bunkaroe left over from when all the cows were here."

A "bunkaroe" was a shack the boys used when the Stuarts herded cattle and was sometimes used during rain storms by the farmers. Missus Stuart, Ole Joe and I sat and waited for Pearl to continue her story.

"A thin blanket was spread out on that old shuck mattress, another one was folded at the foot. The place had been cleaned up a bit. It looked as though he knew what he planned to do. He tied a rope around my right wrist and passed the end out of a knot hole in the wall. Then he went outside and tied knots in the rope so it could not be pulled through. He said, 'Lay down. Be quiet. Don't move.'

"That is what I did. I did wonder if this was part of God's plan? I knew I had not been in the 'magic circle' to ask direction but I had been on my way there. Did that count? Should I be afraid?

"That lumpy mattress was not very comfortable but it was not too bad. The blanket under me was clean and the one over me was also clean, although they both had a slight odor of coal smoke. I closed my eyes and started quoting Bible verses to myself, 'In the beginning God created heaven and earth.' Then I skipped over to the Lord's prayer, the twenty-third Psalm, the thirteenth chapter of first Corinthians. I may have fallen asleep.

"The next thing I remember he was pulling my skirt and petticoats up. He had removed his pants and I saw his thing. I knew then what was going to happen to me, Mama. I have read your books and remember that talk you gave me before my first monthly started.

"I thought, 'He is going to make me a woman. This is God's plan for my life.'

"He said, 'Be quiet, lie still. I won't hurt you.'

"Mama, he lied. He did hurt me. He hurt me so bad I almost cried out. I did not cry out but he paused anyway. I thought for a second he was going to pull his thing out of me and leave me alone. He didn't. He kept right along. Faster and faster then he started jerking and jerking and I knew his sperm was trying to find my egg. I was still and quiet with my eyes closed.

"Then he went outside for while, returned and did a strange thing. He removed my under petticoat and left. Before the sun went down, he returned with it. It smelled like sunshine. I knew it had been freshly washed and laid in the sun to dry.

"Mama, why would he do that? That was a clean petticoat when I left home."

Missus Stuart and I looked at each other, knowing the man had washed the bloodstains out of the material, perhaps in hope he could get away without anyone else knowing about his misdeed.

Pearl told about him returning later with a freshly cooked rabbit and some slightly warm biscuits for her to eat. She said the rope was long enough for her to take a few steps in the building. The food was good; she ate two of the biscuits and about half the rabbit. There was a jar of fresh spring water by her bed at all times.

She did not see the man eat. Except when he was doing something for her or to her, he was outside. He did not sleep inside. Under the bed was one of Mister Stuart's pickle jars with a flattened tin can cover. This was to be used as a chamber pot. There was also a well-worn Bible he had left under the pillow.

Later that night she awoke to feel him lifting her skirts again. She said that time it did not hurt when he entered her. She was a little sore. When he finished he handed her a wet cloth to wash with.

The next two days were about the same. In the time he kept her prisoner, they had intercourse six times. On the second and third day, he fed her canned peaches and tomatoes. She was sure they were some I had canned. Nothing in our house seemed disturbed but I never knew how many jars of fruit or vegetables we had unless they were getting low.

After they had sex the last night, Pearl said, "I wish I was home."

He answered, "I wish I was back in east Tennessee." That was the most she had heard him say.

When Pearl awoke after the third night of her captivity, she found the rope was lying on the floor by her bed. She was free to go. The man was gone.

Later she said to me, "Mama, that knot on my wrist was easy to untie. Surely I could have untied it anytime. Was I just waiting for God to do it for me? Did I somehow deserve what happened to me? Was it God's plan all along? Am I going to have a baby?"

An intense search was made for the rapist. The only clue we had was that a man of that description was seen hanging around the railway station, but that he never bought a ticket.

I did not have answers to her first questions. Later I knew the answer to her last question was yes. Her body started changing. About six months later, she felt quickening. That baby was one of the most active embryos I have ever felt.

Pearl seemed to enjoy her pregnancy. She had a glow about her that most of the time young mothers get. She read her Bible a lot. The same Bible the strange, dark man had left under her pillow. Once she asked me, "Mama, am I like the Virgin Mary? She was a girl like me. Will I give birth to the Savior of the world?"

I answered her. "Pearl, I do not know if your baby will save the world. No one knows when or how the Son of God will return. We are told to be ready at all times."

After Walter died, I had returned to his Baptist church for three Sundays. It was not easy. Everywhere I looked I saw Walter. Some people would cry when they saw me. Others would hold Pearl and say how much she looked like Walter.

A Sunday a month later a patient of mine went into labor and the Stuarts took Pearl with them to the Lutheran church. After that, we went to the Lutheran church. It seemed more convenient and we did not attract as much attention. The churches I had attended have been chosen for me by life. If I had moved to Mississippi with my father when I was ten, we probably would have drifted to a different church. I am sure we would also have found an oak tree for our private rituals.

Other things were happening to the people I knew while I was living my life. When I was about eleven, Greta Muller married

Alfred Bischoff and they later had two sons, John and Wyatt. When Mister Muller died, Greta and her husband inherited the store. Mister Muller owned a growing business as he sold most anything a farm or town family would need, including horse and cattle feed. Seeds and fertilizer, coal oil, dynamite, thread, cloth patterns from faraway places like New York and Paris. After Greta and Alfred took over the business, the town got a railway and started growing. Meanwhile, Mister Stuart built canning factories, coal yards, ice houses and furniture factories.

Alfred Bischoff was a real dreamer. As a child in Germany, he grew up near a castle and dreamed someday he would have one. To make that dream a reality, he started building a new store. He said he was, "building an asymmetrical building that would last a thousand years." It did not. He had two sub basements, a basement, three floors above and an attic. These were built of rocks— some of them really big—and heavy timbers. It was a monster of a store and sat by itself on three acres of land. He was a kind man with a good head for business. There will be more about him and his store later in my story.

Amos, Doctor Johnson's son, finished medical school in Chicago and moved to Arcidia. He had always wanted to be a doctor and live in Arcidia. His mother and father were not divorced, but she lived with her mother in her former hometown saying her mother was sick and needed her. Doctor Johnson lived in his big house alone until Amos moved in.

A romance started soon after Amos arrived. The Lutheran Pastor had three daughters. They must have had names but were always known as Big Sister, Sister, and Little Sister. Little Sister and Amos started walking out together and were married three months later. Missus Johnson came to the wedding dressed in the latest Paris fashion and walked down the aisle with Doctor Johnson looking as though she had been by his side the whole thirty years of their marriage. She had only been in Arcidia at times when she could dress up and take charge. Otherwise, she stayed in her hometown with her mother that Amos said was "a healthy old woman."

Shortly after Amos and Little Sister were married, Missus Johnson's mother was killed while at a county fair. The seat on a Ferris wheel broke and sent her flying. After her funeral, Missus Johnson told her husband she would never come back to Arcidia. He offered her a divorce but she said to him, "A divorce is out of the question. I would be known as a 'grass widow' and would be shunned by all my society friends."

She was right. Widows were petted and welcomed in all levels of society but having a divorce put a woman up on a block of shame. Victoria was Queen of England at that time and in some ways she ruled the world. She was a dumpy woman that changed the way we dressed, built and furnished our houses, chose our mates, held our forks and the way we treated other people. She did all of this without war. That was real power.

Amos and Little Sister moved into Doctor Johnson's house and he became "Doctor Amos Johnson." My workload increased with the town growing so fast and more babies being born. Doctor Johnson built a small hospital. There were, after Amos came, ten members of the staff including another doctor.

Amos had been home about six months and Doctor Johnson had turned most of his patients over to him. He came into my office and said, "Cleo, let us go for a buggy ride."

All of our buggy rides together had been to see patients so I was surprised that the good Doctor was asking me just to ride out with him.

Taking my hand in his, after we had ridden out of town about a mile, he told me how much he loved and respected me. I did not know what was coming. I patted his hand and told him how much his love and friendship had meant to me over the years, that he was like a third father to me. "After my real father and Mister Stuart, you come first."

"Yes," he said. "I know Mister Stuart is still here for you, but he will not be with you very long. We both know his lungs are giving out on him, and that Ole Joe has moved into his house to help take care of him." He continued, "Cleo, I did not ask you to ride with me to talk about the past. What I want to talk about is the future. My future. I am leaving Arcidia. Amos is taking over my practice. He is like you, he wants to live here and no place else. His mother is not coming back and I cannot bring it into my heart to divorce her. I am moving to Utah."

Doctor Johnson had been as great an influence on my life as anyone and I had loved and respected him since I was nine years old. His leaving would leave a hole in my life and my heart.

Crying, I said, "You will be going to Utah where you know no one and there will be no one to love you."

He put his arms around me and asked, "Do you remember Missus Putman? The lady that was with Starr, from the Girl House, when we went to help Starr deliver her baby."

Of course that memory was still with me. My night with Starr had led to me losing my virginity. No woman forgets that.

He continued, "At that time Missus Putman and I had been lovers for many years. She and her young husband had moved to the farm we visited to stay with her uncle while her husband worked in logging. Her husband was injured when a saw blade broke and hit him in the stomach. We did everything we could for him but he died three weeks later."

He looked across the field we were passing as though reliving that time in his life. I did not speak. He continued. "To try to comfort that tired young widow, I took her in my arms. A feeling of love flowed through me that I had never experienced before. Her uncle wanted her to live with him. He had been alone until her husband and she came to live with him. Three months later we became lovers. I bought an old cabin her uncle owned about a mile from his house and called it my 'hunting shack' and spent as much time as I could there with her. The rest of the time, she lived with her uncle and tended her herb garden."

I said, "When we were there, the night Starr had her baby, they seemed so close I thought she and Starr were lovers."

He smiled. "That was a cover up. They do care deeply for each other, but they are not lesbians. We cannot marry legally, but we are moving to Utah together. When Mister Stuart and your money managers were telling you how to invest your money, they also advised me. Therefore we, Missus Putman and I, will have no money problems."

He also told me that Missus Putman was living on the farm with her uncle. She had gone to New Orleans with Starr, but Starr already knew the man she would marry and that he knew her past history. So she had stayed only until after Starr's wedding. All this time I had thought there was no way to keep a secret in a small town, but they had managed it. I had a lot to think about on the buggy ride home.

Since Mister Stuart's lungs had been making him so ill, he was trying to run his many businesses from home with his son D.T. Annie Margaret's husband managed one of their district offices which was in Atlanta. He also had offices and businesses in Chicago and New York—even one in Phoenix, Arizona, that he had talked Jed Bell into managing. Jed's cattle empire had its own manager by this time. My investments kept on growing without me changing my lifestyle. I was still a midwife and a part-time nurse. That was the direction, it seemed to me, that God wanted me to go.

Pearl's baby arrived four days short of nine months after her kidnapping and rape. Missus Stuart, Doctor Amos Johnson, another midwife and I were there to help her. Doctor Johnson and I were concerned about her heart. We had known since she was small that her heart was not strong. She never had the energy of other children. When she did run a small distance, she would squat and take deep breaths. Her time in labor was short for a first baby, twelve hours, and everything went well. I caught a glimpse of the baby, enough to know it was a girl. The midwife and Missus Stuart were caring for her and I was massaging Pearl's stomach to help her deliver the afterbirth. We were all rejoicing as I did the cleaning up of the bed and helped Pearl put on a fresh gown and re-braided her hair.

Waiting for Missus Stuart to bring the baby girl to Pearl, I thought, how peaceful she looks. Her eyes were closed and she reached up her hand to mine. I sat by her bed holding her hand and telling her what a good job she had done and how beautiful her baby was, although I had not looked at the baby. Every mother wants to hear her new baby is beautiful.

Still holding my hand, she said, "Mama, I have done all I want to do."

She never spoke again. She died.

Where was God, my heart cried. Was this His plan when He gave me a flawed child? Was her baby the savior of the world, as Pearl had once asked? Was this death punishment for some sin I committed, my father, Walter, Walter's father, or could I blame it on that mean old woman that was Walter's mother? I received no answer from God.

Chapter 20

*D*uring my numbness, I realized things were being done. Funeral arrangements were made; food was brought; people shared my tears; I was held as I cried; the house and later the church was filled with people who cared. I realized I did need them, the neighbors. The neighbors I thought attended funerals just to be seen were there to share my grief. I found, to my surprise, that I appreciated every hug, pat, hand shake, and dish that I received. Walter's death had not affected me as Pearl's did. With Walter's dying, I felt grief. With Pearl's, I felt guilt.

Doctor Amos knew a young woman who had a baby out of wedlock two months before and was living with an aunt. She moved into my house and became Pearl's baby's wet nurse. Her breasts gave ample milk to feed both her son and a newborn. I also hired the wife of one of Mister Stuart's farm hands as cook and housekeeper for our household.

The morning of the fourth day after Pearl's death, I fell in love. Missus Stuart laid Megen in my arms and we bonded. Beautiful. Most all grandmothers think the same, but I knew without a doubt that I had the most beautiful granddaughter in the world. Her dark eyes radiated intelligence. Her dark hair curled slightly and her golden skin was skin I felt compelled to touch. I was mesmerized.

How could God put this gorgeous child in my care when I had failed to protect her mother? I had failed to protect her from the evil man that captured her in the woods. I had failed to allow Doctor Johnson to use his 'magic wand' to prevent her pregnancy.

Yet God had given me this beautiful little girl. My prayer and promise was that I would protect this child, and if she was to be the savior of the world, I would do everything in my power to help.

Grandmothers are a breed apart. Along with three women to take care of her, her wet nurse, our housekeeper and me, there were many, many others to help with her, the Stuarts, Ole Joe, Doctor Amos, the church people, the town people, even some of the people in town. They all felt responsible for her because they had allowed a strange man to enter their town. After Pearl's rape, any stranger in town was sought out and interviewed by the police.

Megen grew tall and straight. She walked by ten months and talked soon after. Every moment she was awake it seemed someone was feeding her information. She heard that fairies lived in foxgloves, that Narcissus fell in love with himself, that the heart pumps blood through the veins in the body, that elephants never forget. I even read to her in Greek. We had no way of knowing for sure, but it seemed all the information we fed into her little brain registered.

The wet nurse stayed with us for a year before she and her son moved to Chicago. Mister Stuart gave her a job working in his Chicago office, and I hired a live-in housekeeper. Her name was Nettie Lewis; in lots of ways she reminded me of Missus Bell, the housekeeper the Stuarts had when I came to live at the farm with Father. Her grandfather had come to America from Wales. She sang many Celtic songs, danced their dances, cooked bread that melted in my mouth. She was such a blessing to me. I still did my midwifing and part time nursing.

Megen was the child I always wanted. Her favorite word was why. "Why is the sky blue? Why is grass green? Why don't the stars fall down? Why, why, why?"

All her questions were given the best answer we knew or could find. Lots of times I said, "Megen, I don't know. I will answer that question when I can find out."

When she asked, "Why was I born," my answer to her was, "Megen, I do not know. Your mother asked before you were born if you would be the savior of the world. Maybe you will be."

The porch that completely circled our house got lots of use when Megen was small. Her little feet ran around the house for miles. We all ran with her at different times, Missus Lewis, Ole Joe, Missus Stuart and anyone else she could talk into running. Mentally and physically, she was a "challenge." As a child Megen never walked any place, she ran. Later, after she was given a pony, she raced. She was a girl in a hurry. She did not run or ride alone. I was determined not to make the same mistakes I had made with Pearl.

The supervision I had not given Pearl haunted me. Therefore Megen was watched closely all the time. She did not sleep in the same bedroom with me, but her bedroom door was always open and I could see her bed from my bed.

Until Megen was three, Missus Stuart spent lots of time with her, mostly at the Stuart house. When she was not being a tomboy, she was a "lady," not just a lady, but a "Southern lady." Her speech was soft, her manners gentle and she flirted with everyone, male, female; no one seemed to resist her. She even flirted with her pony. Ole Joe built her steps so she could comb his mane and curry his back. While she was doing this, she told him how beautiful he was and how much she loved him. Sure, I know this is just a doting grandmother remembering.

Mister Stuart died about two years after Megen was born. Breathing became such a struggle for him. Toward the end of his life, either Missus Stuart, Ole Joe or I was sitting with him. He refused to go to any hospital. He had turned over his business responsibilities to D.T. two years before. His mind was clear until he died, but he did not die a peaceful death. Watching a loved one die a slow death makes you wish that God would go ahead and take them.

Death came at nine-thirty one Sunday night. Daniel, Annie Margaret, D.T., Missus Stuart, Ole Joe and I were there. Daniel had come from London, Annie Margaret from Atlanta and D.T. lived in the home. Lily was living in the "wilds of Scotland" with her second husband and four children and Rosa was in Rome with her husband and two children. Travel was easy with the train system in the United States but ocean travel was slower and more difficult.

Plans were made after that for Missus Stuart to move to London and live with Daniel. This did not happen until almost two years later.

Daniel, on this visit, asked me to walk to what he called "Cleo's Magic Circle" with him. We held hands as we walked and talked of our lives since he moved to France and later to England. He told me of his brief marriage to Francine, a French painter. He said of the marriage, "It was a mistake."

I asked no questions. Then he asked me if there was any chance Megan and I would move to London when his mother moved.

I told him, "This is my home, this is where my father left me. This is where Walter died and was buried. My heart will not let me leave."

When we reached the oak tree with the circle under it, Daniel surprised me and stepped into the circle. He faced the tree, got down on one knee and lowered his head as though in prayer. I watched him. I saw no Mason jar, no butterfly and no ray of sunshine. I hope he got the message he was looking for. I knew that the message he searched for was what direction he should take in his life. We walked back home in silence.

Death in a family leaves a void. Even though, due to suffering, a death may be welcomed. Mister Stuart's death was no exception. After Daniel left for London, the remaining family became closer; the Stuarts has always claimed Ole Joe, Megen and me as family. D.T. started delegating much of his work to managers. As their fathers before them had been best friends, D.T. and

John Stonewall had played together all their lives and became best friends also.

D.T. and John Stonewell decided they wanted to raise families of their own. Neither of them had taken time out for much social life. After they started looking, it did not take them long to find girls they wanted to marry. Two young women, Sara Peterson and Gladys Boswell, were new teachers at the local high school. They were roommates in college and were hired together, Sara to each English, Gladys to teach home economics. No one in town thought they would last a year as single women. Married women were not allowed to teach in public schools at that time and they were both popular with the younger people.

The courtship between D.T. and Sara and between John and Gladys was only three months. A double wedding was held at the chapel on the campus of their college. Megen, my beautiful granddaughter, was only three but she walked down the aisle with her basket of rose petals like the queen of the Nile. Did I tell you what a beautiful, intelligent, elegant little girl she was? Yes, I guess I did. This was still a proud grandmother talking.

Missus Stuart seemed to be waiting for her youngest child, D.T., to find a wife and start a family before she moved. Sara and D.T.'s first son, Daniel James, was born eleven months after they married. Gladys and John's son, Paul, was born two weeks later. It was "baby time" in those two households. Soon after little Daniel was born, Missus Stuart left to live in London with her eldest son, Daniel. Sometimes people are not fully appreciated until they are no longer with us. I missed her much more than I thought I would.

⋄⊶⊷⋄

Willow, let the people you love know how much they mean to you. Some relationships are long and some brief but they are all important. We can show our love by our actions, what we do, what we say and how we touch. We can express hate the same way. Toward me, Missus Stuart always projected love. Did she feel the hate I had for her when I was blaming her for my father's leaving me and going to Mississippi to his death? I am sure she did. A ten-year-old child, or anyone else, has to work through their own grief. She knew that.

⇢⇛⇚⇠

Missus Stuart's first letter after she arrived in London told about her trip and the new clothes she was having made by a French dressmaker. She told about a special ball gown, green with white ruffles around the neck that she was going to wear to a ball where she was to meet Queen Victoria. She also said the ball had something to do with me. Daniel would not let her tell me what it was until afterward. How a ball attended by Queen Victoria involved me I could not imagine.

During the night of the ball, I tried to create a vision. Visions never came when I wanted them to and if I did get one, it was never, ever what I asked for.

It seemed forever but at last the letter I was expecting from Missus Stuart arrived. It contained newspaper accounts of the ball. Of course, the guest of honor was Queen Victoria but the ball was held to present to the London museum a painting "by the most distinguished Scottish artist, Daniel Stuart."

The article continued, "The ten by eighteen foot painting, 'Cleo's Oak' depicts a young girl sitting in a circle of stone facing a large oak tree; a sun ray shines on her and a butterfly seems to be flying around her head. There is a light blue dated glass canning jar in the circle where you can read MASON Patent Nov 30, 1858. Queen Victoria was so pleased with the painting she was overheard telling the mother of the artist she wanted Mister Stuart to paint a state portrait of her family."

Missus Stuart also sent the newspaper clippings to our local newspaper. Our paper printed all the clippings and added, "Daniel Stuart is not from Scotland. He belongs to us. He is fourth generation American. When Queen Victoria heard his name, loving everything Scottish as she does, she assumed he was from Scotland and no one dared to correct her. I can't think what will happen when she finds out Cleo and the oak tree are in Arcidia, Indiana."

This painting was known as Daniel's "masterpiece" and he became known as the best of the famous artists of the nineteen century.

Time passed and Megen continued to be the center of my life. She spent lots of time at the Stuart place. Sara no longer had the students she had trained to teach so she concentrated on teaching Megen. In writing, Sara allowed no abbreviations and no contractions. The Stonewall and the Stuart ladies and babies spent a lot of time together and always included Megen.

I took a lover. Maybe I was jealous, or was I just lonely? A young doctor came to work with Doctor Amos one summer. He was trying to decide if he wanted to start his practice in a small town and be known as a "country doctor" or if a large city was what he wanted. I was almost thirty-three years old. My husband and daughter were dead. Mister Stuart was dead; Missus Stuart was in England; Doctor Johnson was in Utah; Megen had Nettie Lewis to care for her. I had a feeling of being left out of the lives of people I loved and, truthfully, I enjoyed sex.

Our affair lasted all summer. Our meeting, or mating place, was the hunting cabin that Doctor Johnson and Missus Putman had used. We were honest with each other. He said, "Being with you is better than going to the Girl House."

Having sex with this younger and more energetic man was nothing like the soft, gentle love I had received from Walter. Even our first kiss was not gentle and for sure there was nothing soft about our love making. When we left a bed, it looked like a battlefield. I liked it.

Once he said, "I thought I had found a kitten. You turned into a tiger."

He left at the end of the summer. I hope the bite and scratch scars I left on his body had healed before his marriage six months later. He and his new bride went to India on their honeymoon.

He sent me a knife made of bamboo with a note, "The man that sold me this knife said it was used to cut the umbilical cord of Marc Anthony. I think if I had asked him, he would have also produced the foreskin of Julius Caesar. I told him a midwife in Indiana named Cleopatra should have this knife."

The knife indeed was old and as a midwife I knew that type of knife could have been used at the birth of Marc Anthony but I did not believe that was the one that cut his cord.

Megen developed fast. Once when she was three she said to me, "That man was here again."

I asked, "What man?"

Her answer, "The man with the golden skin, just like mine. Didn't you see him? He was here right after you put me to bed last night."

I gathered her in my arms, kissed her and said, "What do you know about this man?" Visions had always been a part of my life. I also had been told by my father that his mother had them. Now it seemed my granddaughter was following in our path.

Megen said, "He did not even see me. He was talking to an old woman and he was crying. He said, 'Grandma, I have committed an unforgivable sin.' That old woman did not say a word, she just held him in her arms and let him cry. After a while, he said, 'She wasn't even pretty and she didn't seem to care what I did to her. Really, she was just a child.'"

"I did not see her. Was she a child like me?"

What could I tell Megen? That the man she was seeing was her biological father and he was confessing his crime? That the girl who "wasn't even pretty" was her mother? At three, the attention span is short. I started telling her about the two pretty pieces of material on my new sewing machine. "Megen, you choose which one you want me to make into a dress for you to wear to church."

Of course, she said, "I want two new dresses."

Life changes, people change but really remain about the same. D.T. and Sara Stuart kept having boys until they had four. John and Glady Stonewall just had the one boy. Glady had a number of miscarriages. As her midwife, I gave her all the advice I knew. Doctor Amos, at one time, suggested she stay in bed and see if that would help her keep her baby. She gained twenty pounds but still aborted at six months. Why did God start a life he did not complete? Later she had another healthy boy.

I have read stories of midwives who say they had never lost a baby or a mother to death. That was not true for me. Some of my mothers died, including my only child Pearl. Some babies died and some were born missing or having extra body parts. One beautiful little girl had a perfect arm, the other arm was about three inches long with five tiny fingers. One mother aborted a fetus at four months and five months later delivered a completely normal boy.

Midwives can only do so much. They are not God.

Chapter 21

Megen was six and we were together at the home of an "herb lady." At that time those who raised or dealt in herbs were called a "witch." Some people thought of midwives as witches since we sometimes used herbs in our treatment.

Indian Annie came to our area a few years before to work in the vinegar plant. The manager of the plant noticed she was not at ease with the other workers. He knew Mister Stuart was looking for someone to grow dill and garlic. She was glad to take the job. Indian Annie was a small woman. Her body and face had the look of an Indian but her hair was bright orange that she wore in two braids. Mister Stuart's dill and garlic farm was already started. Indian Annie had been overjoyed to move into the small house and take over the care of the ten acres.

She was a little strange; her clothes were different and her speech pattern was different, using Old English and Indian words in the same sentence. Megen was also different. She was such a beautiful child but her skin was golden, darker than any of her playmates. I think her difference is why she and Indian Annie became friends.

We often visited on Wednesdays, for that was the day Annie made a wonderful stew in an iron kettle in her fireplace. I recognized chicken and squirrel, butter beans, potatoes, corn and tomatoes. Of course she used herbs, but I could never quite be sure of all of them.

She was a great listener and both Megen and I were talkers.

Therefore we had learned very little about her until Megen asked, "Who are you, Indian Annie? How did you get here?"

Indian Annie was quiet, thoughtful, then she said, "Megen, maybe I should tell you who you are."

Both Megen and I could not believe she was saying that. Megen said, "Who am I?"

The reply she got was, "I arrived in a cattle car from the south almost seven years ago. If you talked to the man that rents the train cars and the brakeman sometimes they would let you ride for free. There was a small cage-like place in one end of the car where you could stand or squat that protected you from the cows. The word was out that the vinegar plant was hiring. I had a little money, but why buy something you could get for free?"

She sat still as though contemplating her next words. "There was already a man at one end of the safe space. We did not speak for about an hour, then only briefly. He said, 'What kind of woman are you?'

"I had been asked that question before. I know I look different and people are curious. My answer was, 'My mother was a Cherokee Indian; my father was a redhead from Ireland.' He too looked different so I asked, 'What kind of a man are you?'

"His answer was, 'I am a Melungeon from east Tennessee.' We spoke no more. Both of us got off the train in Arcidia. It was five days later that I heard what happened to your mother. Megen, his skin was the color of yours. When I heard the man that raped your mother was either a gypsy or an Indian from east Tennessee, I knew he was neither. He was a Melungeon. I know that for sure.'

When we returned home, we looked in every book we had on people of the world and could find no reference to the Melungeon.

When we asked Ole Joe about them, he said, "Yes, I have heard of them. They live in a small area in Tennessee and have no written history. Indians say they have always been there." Looking at Megen, he continued, "Some people think they are descendants of Portuguese sailors. Others say they are descended from ancient vanquished gods. They have their own religion.

Megen said, "That is all I want to hear; do not tell me anymore. I know what he looks like and that he loves his grandmother." She remembered her vision about the man confessing to his grandmother that he had raped an ugly girl.

We visited Indian Annie's home often. Her cabin had the most enticing smell, especially in winter. On the stove was always popped popcorn, still warm and heavy with salt and butter. She roasted corn, coffee, apples, even her own tobacco for her pipe. She roasted eggshells for the chickens. Chickens need the lime in the shells, but had they been given egg shells, they would start to eat their own eggs. With her tobacco she added an herb from her home in North Carolina she called deer tongue. I was not sure of her formula for pipe tobacco, but I knew she used honey and the finished product smelled good enough to eat. We never talked again about the man she had met on the train.

By the time Megen was in the fourth grade, she was the tallest one in class and her golden skin made her feel as though she was different. Children are not always kind to other children. When another child came into her class that was also different, they became close friends. Jacqueline was as tall as Megen plus she had bright red hair and freckles and a temperament that discouraged any bullying.

Jacqueline had moved from Chicago with her father into a house near the railway crossing. Her father was the crossing guard. In Chicago he had been a railway conductor and was home only about half the time. When he was working his wife had entered a relationship with a street car conductor that lived on the same block. This man molested Jacqueline. When her father found out, he and three friends caught this man and castrated him. One of the father's friends raised hogs so it was a simple operation for him.

No police were involved but Jacqueline's father was determined that he would leave his wife and take his daughter where he would be with her every day. The railway gave him a crossing guard job in Arcidia with a rent-free house. When railway men had a layover in Arcidia, they stayed with Jacqueline and her father. She became their pet. She was taught how to sit, walk, eat and flirt by the conductors and servers from the train. They also taught her how to curse and play poker. There was always music, singing, dancing, fiddling, banjo and organ. Jacqueline had no formal training in music but she had a natural ear for it.

When she played the fiddle, she would race around, dancing, singing, yelling. Her fiddle might be on the floor or in the air and she could still play it. Megen played the organ and sang but she used sheet music. The two girls were a joy to be around even when Jacqueline had one of her tantrums. She was either happy or sad with no middle ground. Both girls were a challenge in school because they were more intelligent than the other students in their class. They both grew up and left the nest. Megen went to Chicago and Jacqueline got married.

Megen acted as a little mother to D.T. and Sara's four boys. She was always the leader. Some of the things she led them into got them in trouble. There was a cedar tree they put lots of loose hay under. The game was to climb up the tree as high as possible then turn loose and fall through the branches to the hay. Megen and the two older boys did this many times. When the third boy tried it, he broke his arm. The youngest boy was then half way up the tree, refused to go any further and had to be rescued.

Somehow they all grew up. When Megen was ten, she started going with me to see my patients. She told me, "Cleo, I am going with you. You helped that woman deliver her baby when you were ten. I want to do that."

At first I did not allow her in the birthing room. During that year, Glady Stonewall became pregnant again. She had so many miscarriages since the birth of her first son that she declared, "This time will be like all the other ones and I am not going to allow myself to hope. Losing a baby makes me feel like a failure."

This time it turned out to be a strong, healthy boy they named Frank. Three months later, Sara, D.T.'s wife, found she was with child. Then Megen became her "little midwife."

D.T. said, "Sara is filling the backyard with boys, trying to get a girl."

That was an old country saying I had heard many times. Sara was convinced it was also a boy. She said, "I am carrying this baby just like I did my boys and I am sure this baby will be a boy."

Megan wasn't convinced and tried to tell that to Sara, who said, "Megen, you may be there to catch my baby. If it is a girl you may name her."

Megen started planning the baby's name that day. She asked advice from everyone. We all made suggestions. Together she and Sara decided on Lois Olive Iris Stuart. Megen insisted the baby's first name be the same as her initials. You guessed it. The baby was a girl and Megen caught it. The smug look on Megen's face when she saw she was right about the sex made all of us laugh.

Megen stood up as tall as she could and shouted, "Sara, your baby is a girl, a beautiful girl."

No princess ever had more care than Lois with a doting father, four older brothers, a mother who had in all her pregnancies wanted a girl, and, of course, Megen. You would have thought she had created the child.

Until Megen was sixteen and Lois was four, Megen spent most of the time she was not in school with Lois. Lois was a little angel, very fragile and ethereal in looks. You would swear she had a halo when the light was behind her. At sixteen Megen went away to college. She stated she wanted to be the best nurse in the world and said, "I have to have an exceptional education background."

Later she stated she wanted to teach the best nurses in the world. By that time there were a few female doctors but she wanted to be a nurse.

Sara's wish was to have the most perfect child in Lois. Her clothes were ordered from France, her music, voice, dance, art teachers were the best that could be found in the area. I knew Sara was meeting with architects planning a palatial house to be built on the other side of town, far away from the factories the

Stuarts had built on our side of Arcidia. D.T. would not even talk of moving. Ole Joe had been living in the "Big House"—the Stuart's home—since before Mister Stuart died. Ole Joe was in his late nineties and D.T. knew he would never be contented living anyplace else. Ole Joe and I were alike in that way. We were both homeless when we got to the Stuart farm and felt we were home when we got there. Both of us never wanted to leave. We wanted to die on that farm. We did.

One cold winter day we received word that Missus Stuart was in very poor health. She had been living with her son Daniel in London in a townhouse. The doctor advised her to find a country place to live. That was no problem as Lily, her oldest daughter, lived with her second husband and her four children by her first marriage in the "wilds of Scotland." This was Missus Stuarts second home. Lily often asked her to stay all year.

The family in Arcidia could not decide what to do. It was really D.T.'s decision. He could not bring himself to leave Ole Joe. I offered to move into the Stuart house and care for Old Joe but D.T. would not leave him. He was really not much to care for. By day he sat by the stove in the kitchen and tried to carve wooden figures as he had done for years. His hands shook so much he could hardly hold a knife. His smile, his voice and his intellect were as bright as ever. His walk was slow, and he could no longer mount a horse. But he could cheer up a room with his stories and laughter.

Someone was always visiting him. One day he asked us if we remembered Nathaniel, the kid that stole a horse and ran off with the preacher holding a tent meeting. Ole Joe did not look at me directly but I blushed anyway, remembering how I had seduced Nathaniel. Ole Joe continued, "I heard the other day that he is a well-known preacher. He now calls himself Nathaniel S. Christenberry. He is really popular with the young folks. His sermons are all about the evils of women. I guess he does not listen to his own speech as his choir director says he has had three wives and has one or two new women in each town in which he preaches."

At night after supper it was Ole Joe's habit to take a nap until it was time for evening prayers. It was a Friday night in late spring. We were all in the parlor. Lois was going to do the reading. She was excited. She changed her dress three times and had practiced her reading in front of a mirror. Ole Joe did not come out of his room. His room was Missus Bell's old room just off the kitchen. Lois said, "Ole Joe knows about my new dress and that I am going to read a special poem. It is a poem he learned a long time before I was born. When I read it to him today, he laughed and then, I do not know why, he cried." She continued, "He must be putting on his new red shirt and having trouble with buttons. I will go help him."

Ten minutes later we watched her slowly return to the room. She was not crying nor was she smiling. Standing very straight and still she said, "Ole Joe has left us, his body is there but he is gone."

Death comes to all. Ole Joe's life had been longer than most of us expect to live. His death was the kind we all wish for ourselves. He just went to sleep. D.T., Sara, the housekeeper and I were sitting around the kitchen table talking before we went into the parlor for evening prayers. Ole Joe's door was open. We would have heard him if he made any noise. Ole Joe's death left a hole in my heart that was never filled.

One month later, D.T., Sara and their five children sailed for England. Before they left they arranged for their huge new house to be built on the other side of town. Sara's house plans even included a ballroom and many bedrooms. She said it was important that she entertain her husband's business associates.

Megen was in college, the Stuarts in either England or Scotland, Ole Joe was dead, and I was not interested in taking another lover. I guess my sex drive had died. Beside my midwife job, I became Doctor Amos' "do anything" person, available for night or day duty.

One simple thing I did one day was make a deaf man hear. After that, he always said I could perform miracles. It did take me part of two days but I cleared the wax out of both his ears. The wax looked like an-inch-and-a-half-long yellow worm. We were both happy and he exclaimed, "Why is everyone talking so loud?"

Memories are moments. The news we heard from the Stuarts was not good. Missus Stuart's health was declining. D.T. and Sara's four boys were sent to an English boarding school and a tutor was hired for Lois. Daniel and D.T. spent most of the time with Lily and their mother in Scotland. Rosa from Italy and Annie Margaret from Atlanta gathered to be with Missus Stuart.

Sara and Lois stayed at Daniel's townhouse in London. Missus Stuart was weak and three days before she died she developed pneumonia. She was buried on Lily's husband's family estate. Later a memorial stone was set in the Arcidia Lutheran Cemetery.

D.T. came home soon after that and lived alone in the Stuart house while tending to his far-flung businesses and supervising the building of their new home across town. We spent time together. He was the brother I never had.

Sara and Lois returned home two years later when their new house was finished. Their English accent was more English than Queen Victoria's. Sara strived to be a society lady. She did not have the natural grace and beauty of her mother-in-law but she developed a style of her own. The guests of her house parties were the rich and famous. Her clothes were from Paris; she traveled with two maids and a chef in her own railway car. D.T. was amused by her and loved her. He said of her, "Sara gave me four healthy boys and a beautiful girl. Anything she wants that I can pay for she can have."

It was a time of growth in America. Railways, shipping, real estate, factories, importing, exporting; the Stuart Enterprise had a hand in developing all of these. D.T. and his money managers were still investing for me. I was still working and did not need the extra money, so it just kept growing.

Gladys and John Stonewall were so different from Sara and D.T. They lived in the same house John's family built eighty years before, a frame house painted yellow with porches on three sides. Two extra rooms had been built on the back of it by John's father. Otherwise there had been little change. John was still raising cattle when most of his neighbors had switched to vegetable crops. Now that the railroads carried his beef cattle to Chicago to sell, he had cut down on the number of farm hands. He was really a dreamer. Most of his time he spent reading, fishing, down at a local store playing checkers or listening to other people talk. He was a great listener; I think he would have been a good writer if he had tried. He seemed happy with his life and Gladys was the perfect wife for him.

Gladys Stonewall and I became good friends during the time Sara and Lois spent in London. Gladys' interest was in her two sons, James and Frank, her husband, her home and her church. Her dresses were all made the same way, a fitted bodice with a two inch collar, opening down the front with six buttons above and two buttons below the waist and a full long skirt. Over this, if she was home, she wore a large black and white checked apron. Her Sunday and going-to-town dresses were cut the same but of a better material. She had five everyday dresses and three Sunday dresses. She often used her apron as a basket. Sometimes it held eggs, corn cobs that she later soaked in coal oil and used for starting fires in her stove or fireplace, or for picking garden vegetables. Four or five aprons hung on the back door. One was stained and only used for picking berries. One held clothes pins, another she used to carry feed for the chickens.

She even got me involved with her social work for the church. How two people with the same background could be so different and still be best friends I do not know, but Gladys and Sara managed that.

Sara and D.T.'s four sons stayed in a boarding school in England for two more years, then transferred to different schools in the northern part of the United States. Sara thought they would have socially and culturally better friends in the north. Their daughter Lois still had the ethereal look of an angel. When the family first moved into their big house, she had a tutor and a dance teacher living in, and a music teacher that came to the house for an hour and a half five days a week. In England she fell in love with horses, and of course D.T. bought her the best clothes and the best horse he could find and had them shipped to Arcidia. Riding lessons were added to the things she did.

This arrangement lasted only a week, until Megen came home from her boarding school for the weekend. Lois was small for her age and appeared fragile but she had her father wrapped around her finger. She told him, "I am not going to stay in this stuffy old house all day, with just a bunch of old folks. I am going to move in with Cleo and go to regular school. Then Mother can go any- where she wants to or have parties every day."

D.T. asked me what he should do. Remembering the welcome I received from the Stuart family when I was nine and the joy I felt being accepted in their way of life, I suggested that she come stay with me when Sara was away from home or entertaining guests. I would try to turn her back into an "American girl."

Megen had told me, "Cleo, Sara dresses her like a little prin- cess and when Lois rides she sits the saddle like a statue. The other boys and girls laugh at her. She is not a happy child. I wish there was some way I could help her."

So Lois came to be my part-time child. For two weeks, Sara pretended to be very unhappy about the arrangement. Then she decided she would use this arrangement to travel with some of her new friends in Europe. Lois' tutor was unhappy in our small town and took a job with a family in New York. So Lois became my responsibility. For two weeks, I did not go to work. Most of that time I spent making clothes for Lois that looked like the clothes the local girls wore.

The teacher she would have at school was a girl I had helped her mother deliver twenty-four years before, so I had known her all her life. She was willing to bring her schoolwork to our house and help Lois catch up with the class she was entering. In English she was ahead of the class, and she knew a great deal of the history of

191

Great Britain but almost none of American history or geography. She thought Canada was an island. Megen came home for the first weekend Lois stayed with me and taught her how to ride with an American saddle and an American horse.

Lois was a wonderful addition to my household – with Megen in Chicago I had been coming home to an empty house. Now quite often I had children, Lois and her friends, that ran around on the porch that circled my house until they were exhausted. Children I could make cookies with, I even made dresses for the girls and shirts for the boys out of the same bolt of cloth and D.T. brought a photographer to take their picture. Among the boys was Frank Stonewall. Frank was a strong, sturdy, very serious boy. Always interested in what I was doing and why I was doing it even when I was working. Once he brought a barn cat to the clinic. The cat had been killed by farm equipment. He asked Doctor Amos to show him what was inside the cat. After that Doctor Amos took Frank under his wing, as his father had me, and we all knew we had a budding doctor on our hands.

The Stonewalls and the Stuarts had been friends and neighbors since before their forefathers left Scotland for America. Frank was only a year older than Lois so it was no surprise that they became great friends.

When Lois was twelve she fell in love with Frank. It happened in an instant. Coming out of church one Sunday morning, she missed the first step and would have fallen down fourteen steps if the choir director had not broken her fall. He was two steps in front of her when she fell on his back and rolled. She would have fallen further if Frank had not been watching her at the bottom and rushed up the steps and caught her in his arms. We could almost see the sparks fly as they looked into each other's eyes. From that time on they seemed to be together all their waking hours.

They married when Lois was eighteen and Frank nineteen. They lived with Frank's family, Gladys and John Stonewall.

Their daughter, Mary Ellen, was born a year later. Lois kept busy during her pregnancy helping Gladys and John on the farm and teaching three and four year olds in Sunday School. She also created a tall grass garden. She said she wanted only grasses that grew over three feet tall, grasses she could see out her window as she sat in her rocking chair nursing her baby. Her father and brothers brought her tall grasses from all over the world. This worked well until one little boy brought her a wild violet plant and helped her plant it in front of the grasses. The word got out and it seemed everyone in the county had plants they wanted to share with Lois. Her tall grasses grew and all the other plants did also.

While Lois was growing up, Megen was in Chicago. Her dream was to be a teacher of nurses. Most of her social life seemed to be with the medical staff.

She was over twenty-one before she told me she had been deflowered. It seemed a handsome surgeon from California had caused quite a stir among the nurses when he came to the hospital for a six-month stay. It was well known that he had a wife and two children in California that he loved very much. Megen decided that he was the perfect man for her to have sex with the first time. They were not in love with each other but they were both lonely. When the affair was over, they would have no regrets. They met in a small hotel. After getting nude in bed they started examining each other.

With a small amount of foreplay, he prepared to enter her. When his penis reached her maiden head, we was surprised and said, "I did not know you are a virgin," and withdrew from her saying, "I cannot do this. You should save yourself for the man you marry."

Megen became angry and said, "You get out of here. I am going to get dressed and go down on the street and find someone that is man enough to finish what you started."

He left, she got dressed and was out the door in two minutes. He was standing in the elevator with the door open when she appeared. He stepped out, took her arm and guided her back to the hotel room. Their affair lasted until he returned to California.

The manager of the Stuart farm and his family lived in the Stuart's old house. He and his wife had five children, one of them a girl about Lois' age named Rachel. Rachel was a very bright little girl and one of the most popular girls in her class at school. In the two weeks the teacher, Megen and I spent trying to make Lois fit in with her peers, Rachel slept over with us for five nights. Two of those nights she brought four other girls from her class to our house to stay overnight.

At first they wanted to hear Lois "talk English" until I explained to them that we were trying to get her speech to sound like theirs. By the end of two weeks, we thought she was ready to attend classes in their school. She did get teased some, but those five girls protected her from most taunts and she adjusted well. Although she did not become the best student in class, her grades were above average except in music. There she excelled. Her voice was a sweet, clear, soprano.

Chapter 22

February 17, 1914

"*M*other Gladys, why don't I improvise a punch bowl? No one will care if it is only a pail we use for milk. It's white with red trim and I can make a basket out of grape vines as a nest for it." Lois looked so serious and pretty saying this to Gladys as they prepared the house for Lois and Frank's fifth wedding anniversary dinner.

Gladys with a warm smile to her favorite daughter-in-law said, "That is a beautiful idea. You always know the right touches to anything you do. '

"Thank you, Mother Gladys," Lois said. "It is easy to do things for you. You were my second mother before you became my mother-in-law." She gave Gladys a big hug and continued, "You and Mama were friends when you were a lot younger than I am. I am twenty-three and the mother of a three-year-old girl, you and Mama met when you went to teacher's school at age sixteen. I wish I had known you then."

Gladys answered her with a tiny slap on her bottom saying, "If we don't stop this gabbing we will never be ready for twenty people to eat the food Martha and I have spent hours preparing. You remember to set the tables. We will need both of our big tables. We will bring in the one from the kitchen. It is the same size as this one. With Grandma's linen table clothes, they will look beautiful."

Lois' mind was on how she would decorate the tables. For a wedding present she and Frank had received from Frank's parents a service for twelve in china. It was the exact same pattern Frank had always loved that John had bought for Gladys on their fifteenth wedding anniversary. The china was all white with just a tiny edge of silver. That made a service for twenty-four just alike. Using black china paint, Lois had painted a tiny bee on the bottom of each of her pieces. If a piece got broken or chipped they would know to whom it belonged.

"I will use red berries and green leaves very low in the middle of each table. It will look a little like Christmas but it really represents hearts for this dinner is in honor of the love Frank and I have for each other."

"Don't forget we will use the red wine John and Frank made last fall in Grandma's punch recipe that will add more color to our party."

The dinner party went well, with much laughter, jokes and well-wishes.

That night, after the party, Frank said to Lois as he disappeared into their dressing room, "I will be right back -- right and ready." .

While he was undressing, Lois lit a red candle, removed all her clothes, covered her body with a sheet and was lying on her stomach with her eyes closed.

He pulled the sheet all the way to the bottom of the bed, leaned over her, gave two small kisses to her bottom and one small bite. He then rubbed her body with nice easy strokes and asked, "Why are you lying on your stomach with your eyes closed?"

Lois grinned, then answered, "Because Megen told me to."

"Megen told you to lie on your stomach with your eyes closed?"

"Not exactly. She told me to remove all my clothes. I decided to lie on my stomach with my eyes closed. What you just did was so nice. Who told you to do that?"

"Cleo did. You seemed so real and beautiful lying there."

Both Frank and Lois laughed. This was exactly the same routine they had used since their wedding night. They knew it would end with them making love.

When they were married, at the age of eighteen and nineteen they had both been virgins but had been well-briefed -- Lois by Megen and Frank by his brother James. Lois and Frank did not talk much during their lovemaking. They were well matched, enjoying each other's bodies in many ways five years before they did not think possible.

Later, Lois pulled sheets, quilts up over their bodies and was ready for their "soft talk" as she called their after sex conversation. Lois snuggled as close as possible to Frank's lean hard body and asked, "What did you think of our dinner? Everyone was there except for the pastor's wife. She was sitting up with Missus Jackson. They did not think Missus Jackson would last through the night. It probably would be best if she went to her reward. She had been in a coma for two days."

Frank replied, "I went with Doctor Amos Johnson to see her yesterday and we agreed there was nothing more we could do for her."

Lois said, "Amos Johnson has been so good to us. You started riding in his buggy and helping him when you were just a kid."

"Twelve years old and he's the reason I decided to become a doctor."

"Just think! In three and a half months you will be Doctor Stonewall! If our plans work out, I will be three-and-a-half months into having our first baby boy." Lois continued, "You asked Megen tonight what she saw in your future and she smiled as only Megen can and said, 'I see three sons.' When she said that you looked so beautiful, somehow my whole body tuned up. My spine went into a spasm. I guess I was thinking of labor pain three more times."

Frank answered, "Megen has been good for you. She taught us how not to have a baby until we were ready for one. Now she is helping us start the new one we started tonight. She has been a mid-wife since she was twelve. You were the first baby she helped deliver, weren't you?"

Lois nodded, "With Cleo's help, of course."

"She fell in love with you then and has protected you ever since."

Lois moved her shoulders as though undecided how she would answer. Then she said, "After Megen said you would have three sons, Mama said, 'Lois, are you prepared for this?' Megen's face changed. Those dark, dark brown eyes seemed to get big as saucers. Her face turned so brown, you would have thought that she was all Indian. Her eyes dropped to her plate and she was very quiet the rest of the evening. As she was leaving, she held me and told me how much she loved me and how much she wanted to protect me. Do you think I was reading something into her good-bye that was not there? Is she going to Europe? I know they are preparing for war in Germany. Mr. Bischoff talks of it all the time. He even advised his two sons to change their names to Bishop, which they did when they went off to Harvard. She scared me; I do not want to lose her."

Frank studied her worried expression and said, "That was a huge punch bowl and lots of cups."

Lois laughed. She wasn't fooled; she knew he was changing the subject on her. "How did our parents get together to buy an Ohio Star punch bowl without us knowing? They even got the same pattern as the two cups we bought on our honeymoon. I almost fell over when I saw that bowl in the grapevine nest I made for that old milk pail."

"It fit perfectly." He punched his pillow.

"We are so lucky to have so much love in our lives. Mary Ellen is such a dear. I can't imagine life without her. She will be so proud of her new baby brother. We better wait until I'm at least eight months along or she will keep asking if her baby brother is here yet."

Early in the evening James and Megen had a lot of fun telling stories of how they had prepared the young couple for marriage.

"Your mama said she tried to prepare you," Frank said, "but you told her things that she didn't even know that Megen had told you. Pastor Young even told a few things about our session with him. We were babes in the wood."

Both were quiet for a while, thinking back over the evening, then Lois said, "I enjoyed our singing tonight. Mama played the organ as beautiful as ever. Mrs. Jinkins taught me to play the organ and also taught me to sing. I really do not like to do both at once. I prefer to sing. I did not tell you about my experience last Sunday. Remember the choir sang "Mine Eyes Have Seen the Glory?" When I did my solo part, 'Mine eyes have seen the glory of the coming of the Lord,' I felt alone. I felt I was dressed in white and when I looked up, I did not see the church. I saw bright white light that filled the church. A feeling of peace spread all over me."

Frank said, "That is the feeling I get when I'm near you. I feel there is an aura about you that covers me completely. We will never be parted. You let me know if we need to work some more on having that little boy. I'm ready now if you'll just say the word."

She gave him two pats on the bottom and turned on her right side. They formed two spoons and in two minutes they were in peaceful sleep.

Chapter 23

*F*or some time Lois had been working on a quilt top. She called it a "memory quilt." She included pieces of material from the clothes of people she loved that they had worn at special times in their memory. There were scraps from the sleeves of the jacket Frank wore to church the day he caught her as she was falling on the church steps, a piece of the dress she wore that same day, part of Mary Ellen's first belly band, a piece of the suit Megen wore on her first trip to Chicago, a scrap of Ole Joe's red flannel shirt he had planned to wear on the day he died and other scraps of material. I do not think she left any one of her loved ones out. She even added one of my treasured scraps left over from the material my father sent me for Christmas the year he died and I later used for my wedding dress. It was a crazy looking quilt top.

The morning after her fifth wedding anniversary party, February 18, 1914, she and Mary Ellen went to town shopping. One of the things she planned to buy was cotton batting for her memory quilt. Mister Bischoff's store was always a great adventure for Mary Ellen. Mister Bischoff let small children pick out a piece of penny candy and he enjoyed watching them choose the one they wanted.

In stores at that time, you went to the counter at the middle of the ground floor and gave the clerk the list of what you wanted. No one knows for sure but something on Lois's list must have been on the top floor.

No one else was in the store except Mister Bischoff, Lois and Mary Ellen when there was a giant explosion. Everyone in town heard it. The store Mister Bischoff had planned to last forever was no more. His body was found in the rubble. Lois and Mary Ellen's bodies could not be found. Somewhere in the bottom of those stones and timbers lay two of the most precious people this world has ever known. Was this what God had planned? A rumor went around later that Lois's destruction was because she had made a quilt top using material from diverse materials, cotton, wool, linen and silk. The rumor said that was a sin. This was based on a Bible verse in Leviticus 19:19.

Poor Megen was the first one notified in Chicago and she was the one who decided she would be the one to tell Frank. Almost everyone in town dressed in black and met the train when they arrived that afternoon. Frank and Megen seemed in a daze and walked arm in arm to the destruction site.

We do not know what caused the explosion. We do know that among the many things stored in the basement was dynamite. The people of the town had tried very hard to search through the rubble to find the bodies but their efforts were futile. Somehow we got through the next few days. Mister Bischoff was buried and soil was put over the rubble of his store. Later a memorial stone was placed there.

Frank spent a lot of this time alone standing behind the fence looking at the baseball field where he had played ball on the town team.

Five days later Frank and Megen returned to Chicago, Frank to school and Megen to teach. After receiving his doctorate, he began working in research at the college. His interest was in herbal medicine. His interest in herbs went back to the days he spent with Indian Annie.

Frank's parents, Gladys and John Stonewall fell to pieces after the store fire. Frank's brother James took them home with him. John died within a month and Gladys died six months later. One of the things Gladys took with her to James's house was the quilt top Lois had gone to the store to buy the batting for on that fateful day. James's wife quilted it and offered it to Frank. Frank refused it, so she kept it. I hope today it is keeping someone warm.

D.T. sold the Stonewall's cattle and other stock for them and arranged for the hired hands to find other work. Frank paid James for his half of the farm and just let it go to seed.

The house and farm where there had been so much happiness and promise was now abandoned. The yellow paint Gladys had selected with such care began to peel. I remember when D.T. bought a paint factory and wanted to test paint samples on my house and the Stonewall house. I told him he could paint the outside of my house any way he wanted but could not touch a wall inside. I came home from the clinic one day and the outside of my house was painted four different colors. The western side had about twenty different colored polka dots. It stayed that way all summer. A man would come by every week and run checks on the samples. Some faded fast. Others stayed the same. D.T. told Missus Stonewall to pick a color she liked and he would paint her house. She chose a bright yellow. Over the years this paint became a beautiful soft yellow. Even in its neglected state it was a beautiful sight.

The tall grasses Lois planted reproduced. Some of those grasses were from places like Europe, Asia, Africa and one that I liked the best was from Japan. Today some of these grasses are spread all over the world. We never know what effect our small actions will have in the future.

There was great unrest in Europe in nineteen-fourteen. A war was declared between the Central Powers (Austria and Germany) and the Allies (England, France and Russia). President Wilson pledged neutrality for the United States. Canada sent troops to Europe to fight for the Allies. To fly an airplane in battle was the dream of many young American men. Canada offered some of them pilot training if they would fight for the Allies. Margaret Thomas, one of Megen's young nurses's husband went to Canada for this. Sadly he was killed in an airplane crash while in training. Margaret wanted to, in some way, fulfill his dream. Women were only allowed to be part of the Allied Army if they were nurses so she became one of Megen's students.

April sixth, nineteen-seventeen, President Woodrow Wilson declared we were to join the Allies in the war against the Central Powers.

Megen and six of her nurses were ready to go into the battle zone to nurse the wounded and they stated they would not be back until it was over, over there. That was part of the words of a popular song of the time. Frank also joined the army as part of a medical team. Within a year, Megen, Margaret and Frank were assigned together to the same medical unit in France.

Among their many patients from the Rainbow Division was a young private from Tar Heel, North Carolina, named Joe Chasson. Joe had been gassed. The Germans as one of their weapons had developed a gas that would enter your lungs. If you did not die immediately, your lungs would be damaged. Joe must have been an exceptional young man for after peace was declared, Megen, Frank and Margaret went to North Carolina for his wedding to the girl he had talked about so much in France. Megen seemed to be more impressed by his horse than she was by his bride. His horse was a retired circus horse named Dan. It would dance when Joe played his mouth organ. Megen loved to ride that dancing horse.

While in France they planned what they would do when the war was over. Their plan was to build a teaching hospital in Arcidia and to name it L. O. I. S. Memorial Hospital. The people of Arcidia became excited about the idea. I pledged my house, land and all my wealth and energy. D.T. was also eager for the hospital to be built in his daughter's memory. Even before the war was over, work had begun on clearing the land.

The main campus was on the old Stonewall farm and my ten acres were to be made into a garden. D.T. hired a landscaper from Japan to design the space. It was still to be my home until I died and my beloved oak tree was to be preserved forever.

I enjoyed being a part of this planning. Even Indian Annie helped with choosing the herbs to be included in the garden.

The Japanese gardener started growing oak seedlings from my oak to be given to the dignitaries that would be invited to the Grand Opening. Then the grade school students planted seedlings to sell to buy books for their library. Even today you can buy oak seedlings in Acidia. I am not sure they are from my oak tree but maybe.

By the time our heroes returned from the war, there was a great start on their dream. While in France, Margaret and Frank had decided to get married. Margaret told Frank she would not marry him until the bodies of Lois and Mary Ellen were given a Christian burial in the Arcidia Lutheran Cemetary. There was heavy digging equipment in town to help build the hospital so in just a few hours, the bones were found.

The church was filled and overflowing for the funeral. Two weeks later it was also filled for the wedding of Margaret and Frank. Their marriage was a strong and steady one filled with love and respect, even though both had lost their first love in death.

In a year their first little black-haired boy was born. Thirteen months later, they had twin boys. What Megen had said the day before Lois died had come to pass. Frank had his three boys.

⇀⇒◉⇐↼

Willow, my story is about finished. I lived a long and productive life. Megen never married although she had a number of lovers. She moved in with me after the war and we both worked at the beautiful L. O. I. S. Memorial Hospital. Reading my story may inspire you to write your own grandmother's memoirs.

Now Willow, I am ready to tell you about the last day of my life on earth.

⇀⇒◉⇐↼

The weather was perfect. There was about four inches of hard packed snow on the ground and the air was filled with tiny crystalline flakes that glistened like diamonds. Megen and I acted like four-year-old kids. We built a snowman so tall Megen had to stand on a chair to roll his head onto his body. We made snow angels and later made rich snow cream and jack wax. Jack wax is made by pouring a heavy, hot, sweet maple syrup over a large hard packed pan of snow. That was a little crazy, for by lunch time neither of us wanted real food so we just ate an apple and two hard-boiled eggs each. By then it was my nap time. This day Megen lay down with me saying, "Cleo, I will lay here with you until you fall asleep, then I will get up and read a while."

Two hours later I awoke and Megen was still with me, deep in sleep. I could not resist reaching over and touching her beautiful golden face. Her eyes opened and she smiled.

I said, "Megen, I thank God everyday for making you my granddaughter."

She gathered me in her arms, held me and kissed the top of my head. Strange for two talking women we were both quiet, just loving the closeness we felt.

About three o'clock Megen got our one horse sleigh ready for a trip through the snow, around our neighborhood. Our sleigh bells had the most beautiful sound. Megen even added another set to the ones we already had on the harness. This was a set given to her at Christmas time by a family named Young from Minnesota.

She tucked a Stuart plaid lap rug lined in black bear fur around us. She said, "The Stuarts are still protecting us." She cracked a whip over the head of our horse and we were 'dashing through the snow,' well, not exactly dashing, until we hit the main road. Then we dashed. Many wagons, sleighs and a few cars had packed the snow on the road until it was just right for sleighing. First we circled L. O. I. S. Memorial Hospital and Medical Training Center.

Word had already reached the hospital that we were coming. Many sleighs started following us. I realized we were leading a parade. I asked, "Megen, did you plan this spectacle?"

She just smiled. There were lines of people around the hospital, cheering, shouting "Cleo! Megen!"

We loved it. At one point we stopped to listen to a small band play "Jingle Bells," then at another point we stopped as a young doctor sang "Mother MacChree," in his lovely Welsh tenor. I was not crying but there were tears of joy in my eyes. After a lot of waves and thank-yous, Megen and I drove to the two cemeteries. First to the Baptist Church to pay our respects to my husband Walter and daughter Pearl. Then to the Lutheran Church to view the many graves of the Stuarts. When I saw a little marble lamb on the top of a nearby child's grave, I remembered the lamb I had requested for my father's grave in Mississippi.

Indian Annie had invited us for supper and it was ready when we arrived. The meal Annie served that night took a long time to cook. Into a large iron pot, she put a whole cut up chicken, a cut up squirrel, a quart of butter beans, a quart of corn, a quart of Irish potatoes and a quart of tomatoes and cooked it for hours with herbs. Annie called it Brunswick Stew. She also served cornbread made with yellow corn with bits of fried pork she called cracklins. For drink, we had fresh churned buttermilk. I did not know it at that time but that was my last meal on earth and it was a delicious one.

We talked and laughed for about an hour and could hardly move we ate so much. When Annie brought out coffee and pecan pie, Megen said, "Annie dear, there is no way we can eat any more."

But we did. We each had two cups of coffee and a large slice of pie. What a beautiful, wonderful last day that was. We arrived home about midnight. Sleep came easy for me. I was awakened about four o'clock by a sharp pain on the left side of my head. Then a feeling of warmth flowed into my brain. The flow was gradual and I knew a blood vessel had broken and that death for me was near.

I thought, "What a beautiful way to die." I felt cheerful and happy. In less than three minutes I was dead.

Maybe not really dead. There is a Celtic belief that you are not dead until you are forgotten. Therefore I will live as long as the garden called "Cleo's Oak" is alive, as long as the painting called "Cleo's Oak" hangs and as long as any of "Cleo's Oaks" live in the world.

Willow's Other Page

∾

It is January. In six months I will have finished high school and be off to an exciting summer. I can't wait; make that cannot wait. My Christmas vacation was spent in Arcidia, Indiana, working as a volunteer at LOIS Memorial Hospital, and next summer I will return to be a volunteer aide to Doctor Jennifer Maranki for the whole summer.

How did I manage that? Last August I sent my maternal grandmother a hard copy of my story "Cleo's Oak" to critique. She called me back at once and told me one of my forefathers was Alfred Bischoff. Remember, he was the man killed with Lois Olive Iris Stuart Stonewall and her four-year-old daughter Mary Ellen in an explosion. She also told me that our family was a founding member of LOIS Memorial Hospital and helps financially to support it to this very day. A cousin of ours was on the board of directors, and if I could bring my grades up she would arrange for me to volunteer there during the Christmas holidays and next summer. I did and she did.

Cleo told me I would be remembered for a thousand years for a scientific discovery. The future only belongs to those who prepare for it. Before writing Cleo's story, my dream was to be a fashion model. Science class was something I barely passed. After Cleo told me I would have a positive effect on the world, my life changed. I wanted to learn. I amazed everyone and became an A+ student.

Doctor Maranki met my plane in Arcidia late at night on the same day of the last day of school before the Christmas break. She did not look at all like I expected. Her hair was short and dark. Her clothes looked as though they were from Paris or Rome. Later I met her new husband, John Bishop, and fell in love with both of them. But this is Cleo's story, not mine. I told no one except my maternal grandmother why I was interested in Arcidia, Indiana. Going through my mind was the question, was Cleo's story true? On Christmas day, Doctor Jen—she asked me to call her Jen; I settled on Doctor Jen—John and I were walking through the hospital garden called "Cleo's Oak" when I saw on the ground a small part of a fallen tree that included a knot.

There were bits of brown paper that looked as though it had been part of a squirrel's nest. I picked up eight of the larger pieces; only two of them had any letters I could read. One said "sippi" and the other said "hate." I knew they were part of the only surviving letter Cleo had written when she found out her father had died. Next summer, I will look for more clues. I can't wait. I can't wait.

Another reason I can't wait is because I met a handsome young man who also will be volunteering next summer. Somehow I was not surprised when he told me his name was Stuart Johnson.

THE END

ACKNOWLEDGMENTS

A manuscript does not become a book without the talents of special people. My thanks to all, especially the following: Maggie Bishop for deciphering my scribble and typing the manuscript, Judith Geary for editing and book preparation, Bob Gillman for cover photo and financial advice, Kerri Clark for proofreading and High Country Writers and other friends for suggestions. My everlasting appreciation goes to Lyle D. Bishop II for his love and support.

24946581R00124

Made in the USA
Lexington, KY
10 August 2013